TOUCH OF GOLD

TOUCH OF GOLD: KING MIDAS' PRISONER

Contact Info: therealshawnjromeo@gmail.com

Ebook Cover by Getcovers (@getcovers_design)

Paperback Cover Haadi E.K. (@artbyhaadi)

Interior art by @valerianrv

Editor: Molly Darling (@darling_author_services)

Playlist

Fairytale (From "Shrek") Geek Music
The Drowning by Elsa & Emilie
Stockholm Syndrome by ARCANA
Darkness in Isolation by Christopher Haigh & Gothic Storm
Masquerade by Euphoria & Bolshiee
Fallen by Kendra Dantes
Bad Blood by Black Math
To Be Loved by Askjell & AURORA
KISS ME WITH YOUR EYES by Morgan Clae
Without You - Extended by Ursine Vulpine and Annaca
Never Forgot by Kendra Dantes
Play With Fire (Alternate Version) by Sam Tinnesz, Ruelle &
Violents
Listen to the playlist on Spotify

Pronounciation Guide

Names:

Onyria - AH-N-IH-R-IY-AH

Rhydian - RID-EE-UHN

Alistair - AL-UH-STER

Thadeus - TH-EY-D-IY-AH-S

Elowen - EH-LOH-WEN

Alexei - UH-LEK-SEE

Elyssa - AH-L-IH-S-AH

Atreus - AE-T-R-IY-AH-S

Seraphina - S-ER-AA-F-IY-N-AH

Helios - HH-IY-L-IY-AA-S

Aurealina - AH-R-IY-L-AH-N-AH

Morpheus - M-AO-R-F-IY-AH-S

Realm:

Alynthian - UH-LIN-THEE-IN

Kingdoms:

Kingdom of Valtain - V-AE-L-T-EY-N

Kingdom of Anduin - AE-N-D-UW-N

Acknowledgements

Thank you,

Jaida, my beautifully talented sister, for fearing Rumpel from Once Upon a Time, I wouldn't have dared to write Onyria and the Weavers' story without you. Thank you for making our childhood the most fun by reinacting my stories; I wouldn't have Alynthian without you.

Mom, I should truly be thanking you for pushing me to become a writer since you knew this was my passion before I even did. I don't think I would have pushed for this these past few years if not for your comment back in 2022. Thank you for choosing Once Upon a Time as the first show we watched when we got Uncle Akil's Netflix. You are the reason I write, the reason I dream of countless fictional worlds; you are my hero, my person, and my reason for wanting to be the best version of myself.

Molly, thank you so much for helping me clean this book and making me laugh with each email. I will never forget how I messed up with the mother being dead and then alive scene. I had to read through my outline to realize that I was supposed to say "father," so thank you for pointing that one out. Now, whenever you read this book, you can come here and be reminded of how I confused myself. I look forward to sharing the rest of Onyria's journey with you and sharing much more of this entire world that is Alynthian.

To my lovely Bookstagram bestie, Taylor: You made this possible by encouraging me every step of the way, listening to my rants, and letting me tell you about all the smutty dark romance and omegaverse books I plan to write when I am old and gray. Thank you for being my friend, and know that any and all future books that are omegaverse were because of you.

To all my other Bookstagram besties, Haadi, Deevas, Reina, Mia, Katlynn, and my co-writing bestie, T.M. Mayfield. You all and your messages are the fuel that powers my creativity when I think I have nothing left to give, so thank you for following my journey so far.

Author's Note

This is book one in a new adult romantic fantasy/fairytale retelling serial series inspired by Greek mythology, following the adventures of Onyria as she rose to power. There is a sexually explicit scene in this book: blood, death, violence, mentions of multiple suicidal attempts (off page), and mention of sexual assault. This book is not a slow burn and does not end with a happily ever after, as it is book one in a serial series; therefore, it has two cliffhangers.

Reader discretion is advised.

To you, the reader

"Don't underestimate the allure of darkness, Stefan. Even the purest hearts are drawn to it."

— Klaus Mikaelson, The Vampire Diaries, Season 4, Episode 17

Prologue

Once upon a time, in a world long since forgotten, fairytales of charming princes saving princesses from hidden towers and poisoned apples ruled the Realm of Alynthian. This is not one of those stories, for the prince does not save the damsel from a dragon, but they just might live happily ever after, one day.

Chapter 1

Onyria

Nothing but the sound of blood dripping to the floor could be heard in my small hut as I skinned the rabbit I intended to put in the stew for dinner. I wrapped my wool blanket around me as I stayed warm by the dimly lit fireplace. There was no more wood to bring the flames back to life, and I feared asking my father to make yet another trip outside.

Especially since he finally found time to rest after the hard few days of not being able to find a deer to hunt. With winter rolling in fast, my father had returned with fewer provisions than three weeks ago when he went hunting in the enchanted forest, so I had to kill my favorite animal so that we could eat.

Tears streamed down my cheeks even after I snapped the delicate creature's neck; no, it did not stop when I peeled back its skin and listened to the blood drip all around me.

I hadn't expected there to be so much blood, it was everywhere. I had used a bucket to collect most of the crimson liquid, but it was small, and now the blood overflowed and pooled all over the wooden planked floor.

I cursed when the dainty knife I had been using scratched me and clattered to the floor. I reached for the blade when a pair of hands rested on my shoulders.

"Let me take over."

My father's sleepy voice sounded from behind me. I shook my head as more tears stained my cheeks. I needed to be strong for him. I had to prove I could take care of us.

He did everything else; during the spring and summer seasons, he let me take care of the mill, making sure we stocked enough flour for the king. Yet, during the winter, he took over hunting, chopping wood, and making sure I never went without a new pair of boots. Though the ones I wore now were leather and didn't quite help keep my toes warm from the harsh winter.

The only outfit I had that was warm enough was an earth-toned dress made of prickly, unrefined fabric. It was workable with its long sleeves and humble neckline. I also wore torn gray leggings for extra warmth when the wind tried to carry my dress away. I used to have an apron, but my father had used it to make the fire stronger weeks ago, so I made due with the wool blanket I now keep around me.

"I can do it," I finally said once the tears subsided, and my shaking arms no longer trembled from my utter useless emotions. I wanted to disappear and hide from my father.

"You don't always have to act strong for me, kid," he said.

I smiled. "I can handle one rabbit," I whispered, my trembling voice betraying me, and by the look on my father's face, and his gaze falling to the blood pooling at my feet, I knew he did not believe me either.

He gave my shoulders a reassuring squeeze, before taking the knife and chunky rabbit out of my hand so he could finish what I started. My eyes widened upon noticing the four very dead, unskinned rabbits in his hands as he handed them to me.

I wasn't sure what he wanted me to do with them, but by the look on his face, there could be only one thing he wanted me to do with them.

"There are many ways for you to be strong for the both of us, my little dream," he said. "Go to the market in the town and trade those rabbits for a bit of coin.

I smiled, not only because he used the nickname he and my mother had used when I first came into this world, but because he was giving me another way to be useful.

"I will be back before dinner, then."

My father, Roderick Blackwood, always told me I didn't have to act strong and that he would always take care of me.

But he wouldn't be here forever.

Gods, I prayed it wasn't for a very long time, but time wasn't kind to people like us. While the king could reach out to the best healers across the continent, he had chambers of endless gold and could live lavishly without the fear of the seasons killing him.

We didn't have such luxury. The people of Cinder Hollow worked to the bone, paid the king monthly taxes, and died when there was no more food to feed ourselves.

That was our reality.

That was the harsh truth of how we lived each and every day. My biggest dream and hope was to collect enough coin to leave the town and travel to a kingdom that ensured we had a life.

I read that beyond the misty Anduin mountains, there were countless kingdoms, ruled by elves, fae, dwarves, and humans, that had extraordinary magic.

That was where I wished to go—to all those kingdoms that promised adventure, a bit of danger, and maybe romance.

Not that I was romantic. The only book I ever read was about a girl who fell in love with a beastly creature after he kept her prisoner in his castle.

I never saw the appeal, but that didn't stop me from wanting to fall in love and settle in a proper cottage surrounded by cherry blossom trees. Children were not on my list of journeys I wanted to go through unless it was my choice, but that didn't mean I didn't want any.

Just not for a very long time.

Getting to my feet, I tied back my long, wavy auburn hair that fell past my waist into a simple braid. I grimaced upon seeing my reflection of the small round mirror hanging on the wall by the only door to the hut.

Dried blood stained the dress's skirt beyond repair, and upon looking up at my face, I couldn't tell where the light dusting of freckles began or where the drops of blood ended across my nose and cheeks.

During the winter, my skin took on a rosy hue, and the boys of the town mocked me, saying if I were to be left in the snow, I'd most likely turn a shade of red until I caught fire.

Rolling my eyes, I made my way towards the front door. I didn't need a reminder that there wasn't a suitable match for me here in Cinder Hollow. It was just another reason to leave and settle in a kingdom where no one knew me or my father, a new home where we could be whoever we wished.

Upon opening the door, a fresh, wintery breeze hit my face, causing my bones to shiver. On days like this, it was hard not to love this season, but by the time night fell, it would be a dreadful thing for one to walk through; one's limbs would surely snap from the sheer cold.

I hadn't noticed, but blood trickled down the necks of the four rabbits I slung over my shoulders, leaving a crimson trail behind me as I made my way to the town market. Livestock was becoming increasingly difficult to purchase with the little coin we had left, so my father hunted when the moon was high.

It's not like there was much to hunt anyway with the new laws the Mayor of Cinder Hollow put in place, now we only come to the market for meat trade. I should probably be wary of coming into town every time my father sent me fresh meat, but someone had to feed the town.

That's what my father always told me anyway. The people are starving and thirsty now that the well has run dry; neither that nor the current season did us any favors. But of course, the mayor has a solution every year for these complaints.

Every year, when the well goes dry and food becomes too hard to track and find, a fae is hunted instead, and we burn them to the stake. No one knows why, but after the faerie was killed, food, water, and all other necessities became attainable.

But only if a faerie dies.

I had no problem watching them burn each year, after the hell I went through as a little girl growing up in this little town, with its peculiar inhabitants.

From being abandoned by my mother and her new lord husband four nights in a row to nearly being eaten by the Ginger Queen, I was sick of the fae, and the torment my people endured.

My suffering did not end there, though. My stepmother died of hunger shortly before my brother and I returned home. When I turned thirteen, wild fae attacked our village, and I watched as my four stepbrothers were gutted alive.

But what hurt the most was my brother's disappearance the day after I turned twenty. The other villagers whispered that I had something to do with it. Some folks whispered that I bargained with the fae to have him taken into the enchanted forest to die.

Some even believed I was a witch and that I lured children into the forest to be eaten, and that my brother found out, and that was why he never came back.

They were all false rumors, though.

I had lived in my family hut just outside the village on the border of the Enchanted Forest with my father in peace for the past year, without the squabbling of nosy neighbors that feared me. I rather preferred it this way, and it gave me the freedom to live however I pleased without being judged by those who would see me harmed.

I made my way to the butcher shop and smiled when I saw my friend hard at work. Contrary to everyone's beliefs about me, I do have one friend in this wretched town.

"Alistair!" I shouted, waving a hand for him to spot me easily.

That boyish smirk I've come to enjoy seeing every day made an appearance as he looked up with those bright amber eyes.

Alistair Frostspire came to Cinder Hollow five years ago with his mother and father to help with the low provisions here. Sadly, Alistair's mother was slaughtered in one of the wild fae attacks last year, which resulted in his father barely coming outside to see anyone.

But even with all the gloom this village brought, Alistair had people who brought plump deer and a few pigs once a month since that was all the mayor allowed. I placed my father's bounty on the chopping board beside Alistair, and he grimaced at them before eyeing me.

"What did those rabbits ever do to you?" he teased.

I rolled my eyes playfully, and sat on a wooden stool across from him. "They got stuck in my father's traps, so I guess he figured they would go nicely with carrot stew in exchange for a bit of coin," I mused.

Alistair made a gagging sound as he picked up one of the rabbits. I watched in amazement as he chopped off their heads and started skinning them with his bare hands.

"You know you shouldn't be waving these around in the daytime, right? I would have skinned them tonight," Alistair tells me. "The last thing I want is for the mayor to have another reason to flog you in front of the people again."

I scoffed. "The lot of them can fuck off for all I care, Alistair," I told him. "Nothing will ever make Roderick or I stop aiding the town to the best of our abilities."

His reminder that the mayor and his cronies were watching me and my house so they could purposely punish me for my father's extra activities was something I would rather not talk about. My father was still not aware of the cruelty the town showed me, and I would like to keep it that way for as long as possible.

The first time my father went hunting on his own, Mayor Terell's wife caught me bringing the extra bounty and reported what she saw to the Paladins that resided in our town.

I was dragged out of the tavern the next day and flogged for all to see in the center of the town. I was fortunate my dear father hadn't come into town that day, or he most likely would have lost his mind. The high priest wanted my eyes stitched shut, but the mayor knew of the name the town people gave me.

Blood Maiden.

I didn't know why the mayor feared the name, but he believed at the time that I was a hero to some and a curse to others. His fear that I would come back as a vengeful spirit to haunt them was, and will forever be, the only reason I could still see.

But that didn't mean he was going to let me go peacefully. No, I was flogged three times for every hunt father was caught coming back from, or for every illegal kill I brought to Alistair.

But I was being more careful now. I sometimes ventured deeper into the forest at night when father went to sleep to check on the traps, even with all the dangers that lurked within, and I managed to come back every morning before my father awoke.

Even if there were reports of me or my father coming and going, I had not been taken to the mayor's home or office in over a year.

Alistair believed it was because they planned on giving me a new kind of punishment, but I thought that the jagged scars on my back were enough.

"What man could ever love a scarred woman?" The mayor's words came back to me. He was right, though. I had no suitors pining over me unless—a shiver ran down my spine. Alistair thought it would be smart—no, wise was the word he used. He thinks it would be wise to accept Sheriff Berrrywick's many marriage proposals that I have rejected time and again.

God, I can see my brother rolling in his grave.

"I am just saying, Nyra, you need to be more careful, or else the High Priest will have you burn like a witch," Alistair warned.

I laughed. "When goose lay golden eggs, perhaps."

Alistair opened his mouth to speak, but one of his eyes twitched as he turned away from me before I could ask what the matter was with him.

I felt a cold breeze run down my spine as the hairs on the back of my neck stood, and everything went ice cold when a calloused hand touched my shoulder.

"Nyra, how nice of you to make an appearance today," Sheriff Thadeus Berrywick said with a menacing tone. "We have so much to talk about."

"No, we do not," I hissed. I shook his hand off my shoulder and prepared to stand and walk away when he grabbed hold of me more firmly.

"*Onie*, is that any way to treat your future husband?" Thadeus asked in such a serious tone that I thought my eyes would melt in their sockets and drip out like burning liquid acid.

The nickname he slurred with his mouth aggravated me. It was a name my brother would call me when I needed to be comforted.

But now, it is a reminder that my father and I were alone, and that our entire family was killed by Fae.

I pressed a finger into his chest before I pushed him into the wall of the butcher shop. "Get it through your fucking skull, *pig*. I will never marry you."

I managed to pull myself out of his hold and storm off without another word. I just hoped he wouldn't take his anger out on Alistair.

My friend knew how to wield a butcher knife, but he was shorter than the other men, especially Thadeus, and had no real strength to land a good punch.

I thought I was home-free when I saw people gathering on either side of me, looking at me and whispering to themselves as more people made a clearing.

I shook my head as my pace quickened before turning the other way, only to find Lady Terell, the mayor's wife, and Thadeus waiting for me.

"What is the meaning of this?" I asked, and dread settled in the pit of my stomach.

Thadeus was the one to step forward, his eyes trailing the length of my body before staying trained on my breasts.

Bastard. I closed my palms into fists. If he took another step toward me or touched me, I would kill him.

"It's that time of year, Nyra," Thadeus said. "You have been chosen to set fire to a fae that has been captured for this year's sacrifice."

A part of me was glad this was all this was, but the other was screaming for me to push through the people blocking my way so I could run.

Even though our blessed land goes back to being resourceful after a faerie was killed, more always come to punish us afterward.

We can't keep living like this.

As much as I would love to kill this faerie, a small part of me wanted nothing to do with this town's cursed troubles, but for some odd reason, I couldn't turn my back on Cinder Hollow.

Why couldn't the mayor just die, along with Thadeus and all those who despised me behind my back, wishing nothing but death upon me?

I'd never be so lucky as to see any of them die. My time was surely approaching; maybe it was today if I refused the mayor's command.

"Can't someone else do it?" I asked daringly. "I don't technically live in the town." I tried to play smart with my words, but I knew I was failing miserably. Even though I live on the border between the village and the enchanted forest, I am a citizen of Cinder Hollow.

I cursed the gods, the fates, and all those who took pleasure in watching me suffer like this; I shouldn't have to deal with this. I clenched my fist, my nails biting into my palms, no doubt making me bleed from the sheer pressure.

To the people, I was cursed. The Blood Maiden. They wanted their harbinger of death and hero to kill the creatures that plagued them.

I hunted animals for crying out loud, and I cut down trees to feed the hearth in my home and was in charge of operating the mills to grind grain and make fucking flour.

I closed my eyes and counted to four. I was not a killer. I was the miller's daughter, for Gods' sake. *But you pushed that witch into her human-sized stove.* My thoughts taunted me.

I shook my head. I won't do this. The mayor was turning innocent people into killers, and for what? Because he was scared of the fae, and their power? Gods, he was a coward and a sad excuse for a man.

"You don't have a choice, Nyra," the mayor said, coming out from behind Thadeus to, no doubt, better see me. "You have been chosen this year and will complete the sacrifice."

"Or what?" I challenged. "What will you do if I do not kill the faerie?"

I knew I should keep my mouth shut, but for the love of gods, these men needed a wake-up call and a reminder that I was not a puppet to be used and pushed around.

Thadeus smirked then. "You will be thrown down the wishing well like all those who have denied this responsibility."

There were murmurs in the crowd now. The people's eyes darted from me to the mayor and Thadeus. I looked in the bustling flock of people for the one person who could possibly help me out of this, but I couldn't see Alistair anywhere.

Maybe that was a good thing.

Thadeus made his way to me and grabbed me by the arm. I knew where he was leading me before the faerie came into view.

But my breath caught. I felt as though I might vomit. Instead of the faerie being tied to the normal wooden stick, he was lying down on a stone table.

"When you are ready, Nyra," the mayor said from behind me.

Thadeus let go of my arms, shoving me forward. I nearly tripped over myself as I saw the normal town executioner standing by the sacrifice. The male faerie was beautiful with his red auburn hair, freckled face, and forest green eyes.

I almost pitied him for what was to come.

It's either him or you, I tried to convince myself. A sacrificial knife was placed in my hand. When I finally made my way on the opposite side of the stone stable, I looked up, praying, hoping my father or even Alistair would come save me.

Neither were visible.

Not that my father would be here. He refused to step foot in this town unless it was for ale and the need to get his dick wet.

Gods, why did I think of that?

Shaken by my thoughts, I was highly aware that everyone was looking at me. Mr. Tommas, our baker, was covering his daughter's eyes while Rosa, the village healer, looked directly at the sacrifice with a sense of curiosity.

Tears began to blur my vision as Alistair finally came into view. He was shaking his head and trying to mouth something at me.

I didn't need to read his lips or hear his angelic voice to know what he was mouthing. He wanted me to run for the enchanted forest and hide out in our secret spot among the tall, red pine trees by the riverbank, where he would no doubt search for me when it was safe to come out.

No one else would follow, assuming that if the woods did not kill me, then the mythical creatures that lurked within would be my end.

But I couldn't run.

Thadeus had walked up to my side now with a wicked smile plastered on his face; he was such a brainless fool. I wondered if I killed him with the knife I held, would his brain process that he was dying, or would he be more clueless than ever?

I stared at Cinder Hollow's newest sacrifice, and as though noticing my staring, the faeries looked up at me. He was screaming in an unknown language and shaking suddenly, and I knew it was his way of pleading with me not to go through with it. I wish I spoke his ancient language, if only to know what curse he was placing on all of us.

On me.

I gripped the knife tighter in my hand as Thadeus shoved me closer to the table. I didn't want to harm the fae as much as I wanted to stab Thadeus in his thick, bulging throat.

But I wouldn't kill him.

Not here, and definitely not yet.

"Aim for the heart; the blade will do the rest," Thadeus instructed, as if I didn't know how to use a blade. "Or marry me, and I will kill him for you."

My head snapped in his direction as I whispered, "I would rather stab myself in the heart than marry you." That seemed to catch the sheriff off guard, and I watched in amusement as he stormed off like the love-sick puppy dog he was.

He'd sadly be back.

I turned my gaze back to the fae on the table and removed the rope, restricting him from speaking and choking the air out of his lungs. I had always seen his kind as monsters, but seeing him now, splayed out like this for me, so vulnerable, I couldn't help but feel as though this was *wrong*.

What did he do to deserve such a fate? Did he kill someone who lived here, or was it purely because he ventured too close to the border?

Either way, now wasn't the time, so I stuffed those raging questions into the pits of my mind and focused on what I wanted to say.

"I am sorry," I whispered, if only for the gods to have mercy on my soul for what I had to do to ensure I saw tomorrow.

The fae laughed. It wasn't an amused tone but rather dry and menacing before he was lying back down flat on the stone table with a look of indifference. "You will all be sorry when the Weaver comes to collect your damned souls for his collection," he warned.

Weaver?

I hesitated to bring the knife up over my head after hearing his words. "What does that mean?" I asked. "Who the fuck is the Weaver?"

He smirked. "Pray you die before you ever come face to face with such a *monster*."

So this Weaver wasn't a fae, but something the faeries must fear as well if this one didn't wish for me to find out.

"What is the Weaver?" I asked this time.

The fae's molten lava eyes searched mine then. As if only taking in my appearance now, he frowned when eyeing my torn dress, which I had draped over my arms.

"The Weaver is death-made flesh," he began. "*He* likes to play with his victims; make them seem important by granting them their darkest desires before taking it all away as you rot slowly from the inside out while he eats your greed and hubris; he prefers it when your soul is already tainted for his pleasure."

A single tear fell down my cheek blurring my vision, and I shuddered at his words. I wasn't sad, but the images that played in my mind seared their way through me as I pictured what the Weaver would do to us.

I had heard what the fae had said but chose to ignore it, until it played in my mind over and over again: the Weaver was male.

This town was infested with greedy souls that were bottomless when it came to their need to feel important and above everyone.

I opened my mouth to speak then, but words failed me as the faerie closed his eyes, preparing himself for the death that would come. "I—"

"Kill him already!" shouted someone in the crowd, and I blinked back the last of my tears as our fate had been written in the stars that would surely watch us bleed tonight.

I brought the knife up over my head once more, and the fae closed his eyes as I brought it down in one swift movement. There was a guttural crack in his ribs as he gasped, and I watched in horror as no blood pooled around him, but instead watched as his body turned to withered leaves.

The air around me suddenly smelled like the autumn breeze, laced with pumpkins and sweet cinnamon spice.

I was shaken out of my thoughts when the crowd burst into cheers and applause as the leaves flew in the wind, but there was no happiness or joy in me to explain the strong waves of fear that had settled over me after killing this faerie.

Something this way came, and I feared I was the one to summon it to our quiet little town, full of evils for *him* to devour.

Chapter 2

Onyria

After being forced to kill that faerie two nights ago, I barely got out of bed. Not even to do my chores, which I had come to enjoy doing. Today was a new day though, as I took my final step outside of my makeshift bedroom, making my way to the door with a determined stride. Today, I would march through town and act as if murdering that fae was not killing me from the inside out, when in truth all I wanted was to curl in a ball, scream at a wall, and never leave my room.

Upon opening the door, though, the sound of echoing hooves coming straight for the town sounded nearby. I hadn't even taken a step out of the door before I quickly shut it, turning back to my father. I cursed underneath my breath as the realization settled in: today must be the day the town paid its taxes, which meant the king was here.

I could have sworn taxes were not due for another week, but either way, we barely had anything to spare this year. We would starve without the necessary funds to buy food and clothes, not that there was anything new to wear in our impoverished town.

It was too soon.

Running back to where my father sat by the fire, I kneeled beside him, my knees drenched in blood as I asked, "What day is it?"

My father shrugged. "The king has come to collect taxes, dear."

Just then a thundering knock sounded at the door, and before I could open it, it was kicked open, and two knights swarmed in, clad in armor, eyeing me up and down before stepping aside to let in a man with slicked back golden hair, which was an authoritative fashion. His cold, calculating, fiery brown eyes that showed little warmth found my deep green with flecks of gold eyes, before I shot my sights to the pebbles littering the ground, and curtsied.

I wasn't sure when my father had stood or when he had realized the king of Anduin stood in our hut, but he bowed as we both said, "Your Majesty."

When nothing but silence filled the air, we cautiously rose, and my blood stilled upon seeing that the king's eyes had never left me; he simply watched me with a cunning smile.

"So this is the girl you said can spin straw into gold?" The king asked, his brown gaze falling on my father, and my mouth gaped.

"Yes, your grace," my father replied, and he didn't dare look in my direction when he spoke, but I knew Roderick Blackwood knew I was fuming at whatever game he was playing. I knew my father was a gambler, having lost most of our valuables to his failed schemes, but an odd realization settled over me as the king eyed me with a curiosity that told me death was near.

Gods, what had my father done?

I studied the king since he had no issue taking me in from head to toe. He wore some kind of heavy-looking fur-lined robe, a dark ruby shade and embroidered with gold thread. What caught my eye was the thick, jeweled belt around his waist and the modest crown atop his head, made of solid gold. His entire body was draped in wealth to demonstrate his power and status among the people of Anduin, though I never knew him to wear his crown when he came to Cinder Hollow.

Not unless...

My father turned to me then but did not speak a word as the king snapped his fingers, and one of his guards walked up to him and handed him a pouch of what I suspected was gold.

My vision blurred as the realization of what my father had done settled over me like a rain cloud. He sold me for gold; he told a lie so he could live to see so many more winters after this one, and I would surely die once the king found out he had lied.

No.

I wouldn't die like this. Not able to face my father, I dropped to my knees and kept my gaze on the ground, on the king's gold boots.

"Your majesty, I don't know what—"

"Get off the floor," my father hissed.

Gone was the kind demeanor he always bore when he saw me; no longer was he the loving father that took care of me, and in his stead was a cruel and desperate man.

I opened my mouth to speak, but before I could retort that this was all a big misunderstanding, two guards hauled me up to my feet and dragged me towards the door.

"I can't spin straw into gold; I can't!" I shouted, but neither the king nor my father faced me. I watched as the king of Anduin leaned in to whisper something to my father, but I couldn't hear past the screaming thoughts in my mind.

He sold me.

I shouted the same words over and over again as the guards took me away from my home, from my father, and from the only life I'd ever known.

My sights remained on my father's indifferent face as I was dragged away like cattle to the slaughter. He did this; he set fire to my life. My own flesh and blood took away my freedom and my dreams. I was going to die come nightfall when the king found out about my father's treachery. If Roderick was smart, he'd pack his things and flee before his grace figured out I was not some witch.

I closed my eyes and went limp as the guards threw me into the king's carriage, but I didn't cry or scream as the fates showed me my inevitable death, because that was what awaited me. I was going to die in the golden palace of the one and only King Midas of Anduin, and it was my father's doing.

Gods, the fates were cruel, but I would see my father burn before I ever willingly let this happen because I would escape, and I would exact my revenge.

That was my promise.

Everything in me stilled upon the king's arrival in the carriage; he held himself with such importance that it radiated off of him.

"You shall bring me a cart full of gold straw by first light tomorrow, Lady Blackwood," King Midas ordered. A dark smile spread across his lips as his gaze landed on my trembling hands. "Fail to do so and—"

"You will kill me," I snapped.

Never in my life did I believe I would speak to a king in such a manner, but if I were to survive, I needed to harden myself.

I whimpered when the king leaned in, his lips brushing against mine slightly. Everything in me curled inward, rotting and dying as he came closer. I sat back in my seat, not wanting my first kiss to be stolen by such a monster.

The king chuckled. "You will wish you died, little Songbird."

Suddenly the carriage stopped, and when I looked out the window, I noticed we were somehow in front of the golden palace. But we had just left Cinder Hollow. How could this be?

King Midas must have noticed my shocked expression because he smiled and sat back in his seat as he said, "Enchanted carriage, it takes me anywhere I wish without the excessive wait time it would normally take."

I rolled my eyes and crossed my arms. Of course, a man such as him would have enchanted his carriage. Eyeing him closer, I wondered what else was spelled.

His crown, perhaps? The odd belt around his waist caught one's eye the moment it glinted in the light of day, or in my case, the dim firelight back in my hut.

The carriage doors were opened then, and a guard pulled me out before I could protest. My mouth fell open as I took in the spiraling gold towers that reached for the clouds. The arched windows, and the angelic statues stationed at the top of each tower like a beacon, all of which had me in awe. Yet when my gaze fell to the floor, I took in the white stone and King Midas' crest of a gold songbird and a silver serpent.

The golden palace was grand up close, though I wasn't given enough time as I was hauled inside. The smell of sweets and the darkened halls caught my senses. Everything was in dark tones of gold with black undertones.

Tapestries lined the walls, and the marbled floor cast my reflection in a new light, and I saw my braid had loosened and the blood on my face and clothes were more profound.

I looked like a mess in a place of luxury, and when my gaze landed on Midas, he was smiling cruelly. "Don't worry, love, we'll have you all cleaned up before you have to present your gift to me in front of the entire court."

My blood froze over his words, and I wanted to break and shatter until nothing was left of me. What cruel things would the king inflict on me once he realized I couldn't give him what he wanted? Would he demand my firstborn or just kill me as payment? Part of me hoped he hunted my father down and hanged him for his crime, but knowing Roderick, he'd be long gone.

I was going to die here. A shudder ran through me as I took in the many steps we were going up until we stopped at a single door.

I hadn't realized when King Midas had left me in the care of a guard or when I had walked up the many spiraling steps of the tower I was brought to, but one thing led to another, and I was thrown into a single room.

There was nothing luxurious about my new, very temporary room. Straw was everywhere in stacks, and a single wooden spinning wheel was by the long, arched window that one could "accidentally" throw themselves out of.

Gods, this was a prison.

There was a stained mattress on the floor with a torn pillow and a thin blanket. The walls were cobbled stone, matching the floor.

I jumped in fear when the door behind me slammed shut. When I twirled around, the sound of a key being turned and locked in place had my entire being sinking into the pit of my stomach.

"No!" I shouted. I ran towards the door and banged my fist against the door. "Please let me out; I can't spin straw into gold; my father lied." I slammed harder. "Please," I whimpered weakly, slumping against the door as I sobbed into an empty void.

Nothing but a singular candle lit the chamber, and I found it poetic that once my life ended, that simple flame would blow out along with my short twenty-three years of life. I wrapped my arms around my legs as I bowed my head and sobbed uncontrollably. There would be no escape from this hell that my father threw me into by force.

I was going to die here.

Chapter 3

Onyria

"He likes to play with his victims; make them seem important by granting them their darkest desires before taking it all away as you rot slowly from the inside out while he eats your greed and hubris; he prefers it when your soul is already tainted for his pleasure."

My eyes snapped open as the words of the now-dead faerie rang in my ears, giving me the sense that death was approaching.

How wrong and right he had been.

Wrong, because no such thing as the Weaver arrived the following days as winter seemingly evaporated everywhere except for around the village and into the enchanted forest. But he was right to assume I would wish death came.

No.

That wasn't what he had warned. He said I wouldn't want to come face-to-face with the Weaver, which I hadn't because it was a lie to scare me and stop me from taking his life.

He failed.

But a part of me wished I'd died with him, for nothing was worse than being locked in a tower that nearly touched the clouds.

I sat there motionless on the floor against the wall, watching as snow entered the tower, making the room colder than ever. Hours must have passed since night had officially fallen, which also explained the drop in temperature.

A servant of the king had come earlier with a plate of warm food that someone like me could only dream of seeing.

But guilt built in the pits of my stomach, and I didn't touch a morsel against my better judgment that I needed to stay strong.

But the truth was that I had no fight in me after banging against the door for hours and screaming for the king to release me from this hell. When the food was sent to me, I'd falsely given myself the hope that the king would free me.

But no one came after giving me a plate of food.

Anger had taken over my thoughts, but part of me felt nauseous when I threw the roll of bread out the window, along with the slices of meat and cheese.

Growing up, any and all portions of food were sacred in Cinder Hollow. The painful feeling of being helpless to give the food to someone more deserving instead of giving it to the wind to use to torment me was cruel and poetic.

I wanted more for myself—adventure and a little bit of danger away from Cinder Hollow—but now that I had it, I wanted nothing more than to escape at the first chance I could get.

Which was why I kept the fork and the knife in the sleeves of my dress, cruelly letting myself hope that when the next guard or visiting servant came, I would strike, but no one did.

No one came.

I was alone in the darkness.

I'd done nothing but stare out the arched window now, not that there was much to see past the raging snowstorm. Maybe I wouldn't see tomorrow with how cold it was—so cold that my tears froze against my cheeks.

My eyes felt heavy, and the internal cry for sleep settled on me like a heavy wool blanket. Gods, I knew it would be best not to close my eyes, but maybe, just maybe, I could for just a moment.

"Now, now, my little *Drithalis*," a man chuckled with a playful tone from within the shadows of my confinement. "Is this any way to greet your guest?"

My mind woke up, along with my eyes, as an alarm rattled through my brain. Someone had entered the tower without me even noticing.

Had I gotten so weak already?

Doing my best to calm myself, I inhaled a breath and then exhaled before I focused on the memory of the voice; it didn't sound like King Midas or one of his two guards he had ordered to drag me here.

Just then something shifted in the dark; a tall, menacing frame blocked out the view of the window. Only the starlit eyes of twilight illuminated the chamber as the one candle was snuffed out. Shadows swirled along the figure as he approached. My body trembled in horror in fear, as I placed my palms on the ground for a sense of grounding, but even my hands gave way to shaking.

I shook my head, slowly rising to my feet on wobbly legs. I was not going to die now, not here, and not by whatever hallucination I had conjured to frighten myself awake.

The shadow chuckled then. "I am not a figment of your imagination, foolish mortal," and just then, a blade of pure obsidian steel came for my neck with a striking sting as the demon trapped me against the door. "For I am very real and have come to collect."

The shadows receded as a stunning male stood before me with midnight black hair that fell in soft curls above his brows with a slight sheen that gave it an almost otherworldly quality.

Piercing, ice-blue eyes glinted in the darkened room as if he could see nothing and everything beyond my soul.

He'd come to collect, and my damnation was his chosen prize, for the Weaver sought only one thing from me, and it was the promise of devouring my soul. Something hummed to the surface of his skin, and I could have sworn his wintery blue eyes darkened to a black hue with a faint glimmer of gold, like that of a god preparing to strike with his full power.

Everything about this male was beautiful; he was crafted to be the embodiment of a god. His pale skin was flawless, looking as though it were touched by any sunlight; his complexion was without blemish, with sharp, angular features that gave him a distinct and almost Celestial appearance.

He didn't look Fae, but his ears were pointed, his skin was enchantingly flawless, and his otherworldly magic pulsed violently between our bodies, which I hadn't realized were perfectly pressed together until now.

But something about him screamed *danger*. He wasn't Fae; I was certain of that now, but something much older and powerful, almost godlike, but his divinity wasn't showing.

"What are you?" I asked.

The Weaver simply looked at me, his indifferent expression giving nothing away as he played with a lock of my auburn hair.

"I am many things, foolish mortal," he started. "I am immortal, a killer, a monster, a demon, tired, hungry, bored, and enraged; need I go on, *Drithalis*?" The Weaver stared me down like I was nothing but trash to him, a bug beneath his boot for him to squash.

"You aren't of this world," I said with a shaking breath. "Twilight sparkles in your eyes, but there is no warmth to be found near you."

I shook my head. What was I saying? These were my words. I didn't know this male, but his presence, his aura, and his demeanor towards me as he watched me with a calculating gaze brought forth questions. Who was the Weaver and why did the fae I killed seem to fear this immortal?

He was immortal; the Weaver confirmed it, but did that mean he was indestructible like the gods, or was there a weapon that could kill him or even immobilize him? I wouldn't die in his hands. I would fight my way out of this room before I let him lay a hand on me.

"You're very brave for someone who was warned about me," he taunted. "I could snap your neck before you screamed for help, sever your spine before you took your next step; you have no power here," he said, and each word was a lethal lashing to my very soul.

I would fight.

"No," he mused with a devilish grin. "You will die because, like all mortals, you are weak, useless, pathetic, and easy target practice, if I do say so myself."

"Bastard."

I lifted my hand to strike him when he caught it, and I was suddenly pinned to the door behind me. Tears pricked the corners of my eyes as he demonstrated how weak I was in a matter of seconds.

"I'll tell you what, though," he drew out the last word. "Play the game the fates have weaved for you foolish mortal, and I might just let you and only you live."

Only me?

What did he mean? But I knew the answer to his words before he had the chance to say it. The fae warned me that Cinder Hollow would suffer—not just me, but, oh gods, Alistair and his father were innocent; countless children lived in Cinder Hollow and were innocent.

"You killed them all," I said, and each word hit worse than a lashing the mayor had ever given me. The Weaver had slaughtered my entire town because of what I was forced to do; innocent people died because greedy monsters wanted to be warm.

"I did, and I took so much pleasure in bathing in the blood of your town, but I will let you in on a secret," he said, leaning in. "I let the children go with your friend, Alistair, for his soul is pure, and I expect great things from him in the coming decades."

I closed my eyes. Defeat weighed me down, clawed at my heart, and cleaved it out. Even though he let the children go, he condemned countless innocent people to death.

"You're a monster," I seethed.

He laughed then. "I already told you, I am many things, and a monster is one of them, *Drithalis*."

That word again. "What does that mean?"

The Weaver looked at me confused until his lips perked into a sly smirk. "One day, I will let you know, but for now, your soul belongs to me," he growled, and I recoiled back in fear.

What would he do to me? What was he planning to do to me once he was done with me—cast me down to Tartarus, or would he keep me prisoner like Midas was doing to me now? Clearly, the Weaver wanted me alive for something, just like Midas wanted gold straw from me.

Something I couldn't give him and would soon die for. Would the Weaver put me out of my misery if I asked him to?

"No," he answered abruptly.

How did he do that? Could he hear my every thought as if I were speaking to him out loud, when I was certain I just stared at him like he was a god to be worshiped?

Oh gods.

I shook my head. "Stay out of my head."

"Think less then; it does you no good anyway; you are one of the dumbest mortals I have ever met," he told me with so much certainty that something cracked in my heart.

"Fuck you," I hissed when nothing else came to mind. I could admit I was naive when it came to the world outside of my town, but I wasn't downright stupid.

What was going on with me? Why did I care what this vile man thought of me? I was strong, I knew how to hunt, and I knew where to strike.

Gods! How could I be so stupid? He was immortal, but that didn't mean he couldn't die like the rest of us.

He seemed to realize where my thoughts had gone, or maybe he heard everything I was thinking still, but I no longer cared.

If I was going to die, it would be on my terms, and no one, not Midas, not the Weaver, nor the fucking people in Cinder Hollow that were now dead, would tell me otherwise. What was I saying? The dead didn't want anything; therefore, they already couldn't tell me what to do.

The steak knife slipped from my sleeve with the next breath I took, as I didn't hesitate to stab him, not when he missed to grab my other wrist or when the knife broke through his throat.

He gasped as I twisted the jagged knife, and I smiled when he dropped to his knees. I watched as he bled in front of me, blood pooling around my feet.

"It would seem you underestimate me, Weaver," I said in triumph, but it quickly faltered when his body burst into shadow tendrils that snaked around my legs and up my waist until I was in the air and slammed into the wall opposite the door.

"I must applaud you, foolish mortal," the Weaver mulled over as he observed me from the shadow of the tower chamber. Nothing but his twilight eyes were visible, with gold rimming his irises as he stepped into the light. I gaped when four balls of flame illuminated the chamber and floated into the corners of the diamond-shaped space. "I truly didn't believe you had it in you to stab me," he trailed off as he stared at the now-fallen blade. "And with a steak knife no less," he smiled then, feigning heartbreak as he pressed a hand to his stone-cold heart.

"Impressed, you sadistic bastard?" I asked.

"Just a little, and that is why I am more than sure you will survive my little game," he said, clasping his hands behind his back as he strolled closer to me. "I will grant you one wish in exchange for the thing you value most."

"And if I desire not to play your games?" I inquired, not in the mood to play when he had bested me not once but twice.

He kept proving that I was pathetic when it came to facing him head-on, and it put an acidic and sour taste in my mouth that rotted my insides.

I had tried to kill him.

I am not a violent person; I don't wish harm on others, but he aggravated me and pushed me to do it.

"He likes to play with his victims; he makes them seem important by granting them their darkest desires before taking it all away as you rot slowly from the inside out while he eats your greed and hubris; he prefers it when your soul is already tainted for his pleasure."

That's what he was doing. Clawing his way through me to find the corruption in me, in my very soul, before he convinced me to play his game so he could give me a false sense of importance.

He wanted to break me.

"You will, and I will take great pleasure in putting you where you belong, *Drithalis*," he promised.

"And where is that?" I asked; my words were too flirtatious for my own good, and I felt limp all over as he drank me in before his icy gaze snapped to mine.

He took my chin in his fingers and leaned in, our lips brushed together slightly as he said, "play with me and find out," he dared.

I gritted my teeth. One wish, and I could be free of this place. One word or many, and I could be free; I'd still be bound to whatever he wanted of me.

But if I played smart, I could survive him too. My gaze landed on the many straws that scattered across the floor; the same straw Midas wanted turned into gold.

Maybe I could kill two birds with one stone. Give King Midas the gold he desires to win my freedom the right way, but I'd still have to give up the thing I love most.

The Weavers shadows receded, and I landed on my feet, my hand pressed to the chain around my neck, until I grazed the pendant. The only thing I had was what my mother gave me before she left me with my father.

I never took it off.

Some people had said I should blame her for the cruelty I faced in Cinder Hollow. I knew my brother did, and he still did to the day he disappeared.

But I never blamed her; more so, I envied her. She escaped when she had the chance and didn't hesitate. Sure, that meant leaving her children behind, but she had gotten her opportunity to be free of a place that was slowly crumbling around her.

The Weaver smirked. I knew he heard my answer before letting it settle on my soul. "So what do you say, *Drithalis*, ready to make a deal with the devil?"

I unclasped the chain around my neck and squeezed tightly on it before I handed it over to the demon I knew I had sold my soul to. Our hands lightly grazed each other before he pulled away, but an electrical current went through my entire being and made my heart race faster than the snowstorm outside.

"As if I truly had a choice," I said to the Weaver and he smiled.

"You didn't, love, but I commend you for believing you did for as long as you did," he teased, and his aura pulsed a violent crimson around him.

What was he?

The hand that had taken my necklace pulsed a vibrant green and then gold as my only good and tangible memory of my mother faded away like the sands of time. My eyes widened upon noticing the gold quill in his hand with a jar of ink.

"What is that?" I asked.

The Weaver smiled, and with the flick of his other wrist, gold mist turned into a scroll, which he slowly unraveled, and I knew he was playing with my patience.

The anticipation of knowing what he planned scorched my skin with terror as I thought of the many things this scroll could entail.

"This is our contract, foolish mortal, in that it ensures that none of my laws or yours"—he rolled his eyes at that last part. "Let's just say things would be quite nightmarish if these laws were broken during our time together, so read up and sign the dotted line."

He handed me the golden contract, and I skimmed it, not finding anything I read to be of any importance until my eyes widened in horror.

"What is this about my body being yours to do with as you please?" I asked. Suddenly, the urge to hand him back the contract was stronger than a tidal wave threatening to drown me. "I refuse; take your fucking deals and games and—"

"Calm down, *Drithalis*," the Weaver said. "I don't plan on bedding you," he said, eyeing me up and down before our gazes met, and I saw nothing but mischief in his starlit eyes. "Though it would be amusing to see you wrap those pretty lips around my cock."

"Shut up!" I screamed. I refused to listen to any more of this. I'd rather plan my own execution than ever lay with him.

"Don't be dramatic, love; it was just a jest. Now sign the contract so you can make your wish," he said, while holding out the contract in front of me with the quill in his other outstretched hand.

"Why are you doing this?" The question slipped from my lips before I could truly decipher what I wanted to hear or what I knew to be the reason he decided to play this awful game with me.

I had nothing. I was nothing and would never have anything more of value to him in the future if he decided that my necklace wasn't enough.

"Because, *Onyria*, one day you will give me something more valuable than the sun and moon, and you might even look back on this day and thank me," he answered with such certainty. I wasn't sure if I could or would argue against him. Maybe I simply didn't focus on the bigger picture after hearing him say my name.

It came out of his lips so smoothly; it sounded right, felt right, and made my legs tremble slightly. How would I best this man at his own game when he drew out dark thoughts and made me want things I shouldn't with his tempting voice of sin and seduction?

I had to, though. I needed to not only best him but also escape him. From my little observation and attention to his words, I understood two things to be true about the Weaver.

He could hear thoughts when one wasn't focused on keeping their mental walls up, which I had done after realizing I couldn't kill him, and then there was his knowledge of things that had not yet come to pass.

He let my friend Alistair live because he would one day do something worthy of the Weavers attention, and then his comment about me.

What could I possibly attain that would be more valuable than the sun and moon? I am a miller's daughter, and I packed bags full of flour for Cinder Hollow.

I had nothing, and was nothing special.

I eyed the contract he still held out to me and grabbed it out of his grasp. I had nothing left to lose, so what was the big deal anyway?

What would I have to be so frightened about that my gut twisted at the thought of signing a piece of paper I could shred to smithereens later?

"Let me make one thing clear, *Weaver*," I started saying before taking the quill, dipping the tip into the jar of ink, and then signing my name on his gilded contract. Leaning forward, I blew on the paper to quickly dry the ink before rolling up the one thing that tethered us together. "My body and soul do not belong to you no matter what happens, and if you so much as try anything, I will throw myself out that window."

I pointed to the window in question before meeting his stunned gaze. I wasn't sure what shocked him more—the fact that I signed his stupid contract or that I declared I'd rather kill myself than be his puppet.

Either way, I didn't care. What was done was done, and there would be no escape from what I had done.

"Well then," he said, clearing his throat, and the contract disappeared in a cloud of gold dust before he leaned in and whispered into my ear, "What is it you desire, Onyria?"

Chapter 4

Onyria

Dawn was soon approaching, and with it, my fate would be decided in front of the entire court of Anduin. I would be at the mercy of King Midas while he inspected the gold straw that the Weaver had begun to produce, using the spinning wheel.

He had spun straw into gold; an entire pile worth of gilded silk was at my feet while I tried to organize the Weavers work. Every now and then, when I glanced in his direction, I found him either deep into what he was doing or looking back at me before cutting his gaze away.

It was strange having him help me while I simply piled up the silky strings of gold into neat piles I could place in buckets for when I presented them to the king. It was an understatement to say that I was nervous about the events that were to occur soon.

My hands were shaky and sweaty at times of sorting through normal straw and the ones transformed by the Weavers magic. I found that pacing around the *warm* and soothing chamber when organizing no longer helped ease the fear that perhaps I had used my one wish stupidly.

I could have asked for anything.

"Indeed, you could have asked for eternal fortune or the head of *Rhydian*," the Weaver said, his eyes never leaving the spinning wheel while he worked.

Lifting a finger at him, I mumbled to myself as I walked towards the open, arched window. Thunder rumbled in the distance, and storm clouds covered the moon's glimmering light. It had finally stopped snowing mere moments ago, when another storm was slowly starting to roll in. Droplets of rain hit my face as I looked up and closed my eyes, enjoying the feel of it.

"Whose Rhydian?" I asked, crossing my arms.

I didn't need to turn around to know the Weavers gaze had finally shifted to me; I could feel his icy gaze burning holes in the back of my head, when I repeated the name he had said.

"Rhydian is the one who keeps you in his little stone cage, but you and the rest of the realm know him by Midas, the one who is blessed with the *touch of gold*," the Weaver explained, and only then did I turn to him with my mouth gaping as my eyes widened.

King Midas had another name.

Rhydian.

It sounded charming for a man who seemed cold-hearted, but perhaps I had judged him in the moment of my imprisonment in this diamond-shaped chamber.

What the Weaver said, though, was intriguing at best. "So the rumors are true; Midas can turn whatever he touches into gold," I murmured.

Then why does he want me to prove I could spin straw into gold?

The Weaver chuckled darkly then. "Foolish mortal, ask not questions you do not want the answers to."

I glared at him. My body felt as though liquid fire coursed through my veins as I pinned my sights on the demon that held my soul in the palm of his hands.

"If you are going to listen to my private thoughts, then answer the fucking question," I demanded.

The Weaver stopped what he was doing with the spinning wheel and turned to face me completely with those icy orbs of his that seemed to melt away a piece of my fury.

Gods dammit.

He was beautiful; there was no denying it, but he was the enemy, a monster, and only desired one thing from me.

My soul shattered.

I blinked once to the remnants of shadows swirling in the air like dancing ribbons, and upon blinking twice, a cold hand wrapped itself around my neck and the Weaver stood in front of me.

My steps faltered as the Weaver strode forward, and a scream lodged itself in my throat when my next step met nothing but air.

For someone who spoke of killing an entire town for killing a faerie, and then making bargains with me for some twisted ulterior motive, his hold around my throat was gentle. But the intent behind why and what he was doing said other things that made my skin crawl.

"You think you are *owed* an answer, *Drithalis*?" He inquired, his fangs bared out for me to see as he dangled my life on a thin thread that he could sever at any moment.

"Yes," I bit out.

I stayed calm, remembering that we had a deal, and no harm could come to me unless he wished to suffer the consequences of his laws.

Whatever those were, I pondered for myself.

He laughed. "So brave." He leaned in and inhaled, his nose brushing against my neck, and I no longer felt the need to fight him. "So foolishly brave, I might just give you what you want."

His touch brought forth a need I hadn't wanted to acknowledge, but with him so close, his lips nearly meeting mine, I couldn't ignore the dark temptation whispering in my ear.

I knew I should fight. I needed to fight him—his touch, his presence—that drove my mind to insanity. Ever since he uttered his first words in this prison, which was once full of dread and a deadly chill.

His magic had warmed the chamber. The Weavers flames that he had placed in the corners never wavered from the harsh wind, nor did the one by the window snuff out from the thrashing rain.

He had done all that for me when he didn't need to. The deal was my necklace for his talents to fulfill King Midas' wish for golden straws. The Weaver had no reason to keep me comfortable and warm against the chill of winter, especially not when his blue eyes did it now.

I shook my head. Thoughts of the Weaver were dangerous and would certainly get me killed, so it was best I contained whatever it was that drew me to him. I chose this; I decided I could live with this bargain, and now I had to live with whatever consequences came my way, no matter the cost.

"Why does Midas wish for me to give him golden straw when he could do it himself?" I asked, our eyes locking as dark blue lightning illuminated his face.

The Weavers eyes dropped to my lips before meeting my gaze once more. "It is said that when a maiden spins straw into gold, it is she who will marry Midas, and their love will lift his curse or doom them both."

It was my turn to laugh. Surely this was another jest because, for one, I wasn't the one using the spinning wheel to turn the straw into gold; it was the Weaver. Then there was the simple truth that everyone seemed to forget: I had no magic.

I couldn't be this maiden that the Weaver spoke of, mostly because I would never stoop so low as to marry the king who put me in a cage so he could free himself of a curse.

But the fates were cruel, and this could be one big game for them. The Weaver already confirmed he could see the future, or at least pieces of it.

If I asked him the question on my tongue, would he give me the answer I sought, or would he give me a riddle like an Oracle would? For all I knew, this all led to my demise, and the Weaver simply lied so I could make a fool of myself in front of the King and his court.

I need to play this smart, I thought to myself.

I met the Weaver's awaiting gaze then. "If I present the straw to the king, what will happen?" I asked.

The Weavers eyes darkened, as if not entirely enjoying the question or perhaps the answer to my burning thought now that it had been spoken out loud.

"I require so much more than a simple necklace then," he replied.

I raised a brow at him, momentarily confused by his words, until I pondered them and realized what he meant with a sickening drop in my stomach.

"What do you want?"

Gods, the way his gaze roamed my body should have been sin incarnate, but it brought to life a thrill I hadn't experienced since my first venture into the enchanted forest alone.

The Weaver leaned in, and the scent of him sent my body on overdrive—a blend of smoky oud and leather, with subtle hints of black pepper and amber. I hadn't realized how dark it was when he first arrived, but now I could see him more clearly, and he was way taller than I assumed and, by the looks of him, muscular.

He wore a black, fitted, cloak that seamlessly blended with the shadows around us. From what I could see, he had on a black tunic with silver embroidery on the cuffs and collar. His trousers were dark and tailored as well, tucked into knee-high boots made of flexible black leather.

His breath against my neck sent delightful shivers down my spine, and I unintentionally gripped at the collar of his cloaks for support, or to pull him closer, I could not say.

"Let me have you in every way *I* desire," he said, a mischievous voice, his smile lacing his lips, pressing light kisses to my throat. "Touch yourself for *me*," he whispered into my ear. I felt his cock straining against my thigh, and the scent of our arousal mingled in the air around us.

Fuck.

This is so wrong.

But it felt so right. I pressed my thighs together for more friction; control slipped out of my grasp as I listened to my raging thoughts that told me I needed his mouth to devour me until words were impossible; I wanted his tongue to taste me in ways I knew only he could satisfy me.

"What?" I asked when I registered what he said, and maybe it was for me to wake the fuck up and realize where my mind had momentarily wondered.

My thoughts were in such a fog that I had only taken in what he wanted me to do now and what I had been willing to say yes to. "I don't understand what you are asking," I stuttered on my words, feigning innocence, but nearly choking on the air I breathed.

He chuckled.

"I said," the Weaver paused, taking a step closer to me, trapping me between the door and his body. When had we moved from the window? Something about this should have had me scared or worried, perhaps, but I felt safe in his presence, and at peace.

Gods, something truly was wrong with me. I am losing the battle against my body and the war of wills against this man, who thrived on luring out the darkness of his victims.

"Touch yourself for me; I want you to imagine that it is me you feel; I want you to taste yourself, think of me, and desire only me. I want you so broken from your need for me, my fingers..."

There was another pause as his lingering, icy gaze found its way to my lips. "Think of how raw I will fuck you with my cock, and where I'll fuck you first. Think of all the pleasure only I can, and will, grant you until you beg me for what *you* truly want from me."

"I don't understand," I breathed, but I did and chose to ignore the excited hum in my chest and the fluttering in my stomach as my legs weakened.

The Weaver smiled. "You do, and when you are ready to admit it, summon me, and I shall appear to give you what you want."

The fog over my mind began to fade as the Weaver appearance crumpled into shadow, leaving me in the tower chamber alone and with the piles of golden straw.

My eyes widened then. He had finished and now left me without the answers I truly wanted, but as my mouth opened, a different kind of light bathed the chamber in warmth.

I turned to the window and watched in both awe and horror as the storm broke to reveal the sun rising to a new day. There would be no more delay of the inevitable now; I would stand before the King and his court while he cast his verdict.

I whispered a prayer to the gods as I stood there like a statue, staring at the new dawn I was witnessing. "Gods, protect me, for I walk a dangerous path, and grant me safe passage into the otherworld for when my soul no longer walks this one."

Chapter 5

Onyria

"When attending court, hold your head high; hands should be clasped together in front of you, my lady, and speak not when spoken to until the king allows it," one of the maids instructed.

Elowen had entered the chamber with four gowns for me to choose from, each one more exquisite in design than the last with rich silk I'd never dreamed of wearing.

When I asked for something more simple, like the dress I had come to the golden palace in, Elowen frowned and said it wouldn't be wise to do such a scandalous thing in front of the court.

So I stared at the gowns, puzzled by why the king and his servants found it important that I felt like I belonged here.

Could Midas believe I am his prophesized bride?

I wondered if others knew of his other name. *Rhydian.* Would he sever my head from my shoulders if I dared to say it to him at breakfast?

Oh yes, I would, since he decided it would be amusing to see me before I stood before his gilded court to be humiliated when he realized I wasn't the one.

I was a fraud.

I didn't even want to marry him; I just wanted my freedom and to escape the Weaver, and whatever it was he wanted from me once this was all over.

I shook the thoughts out of my mind. It was absurd to believe in such things when I was a commoner from a town the king rarely visited unless it was to collect monthly taxes, and even then, he rarely came to those and had one of his servants do it.

Gods, maybe I should have asked the Weaver to take me away from here. Nerves had quickly spun out into an utter storm of fear by the time I was done bathing. I smelled a melodic blend of moon roses and amber, which reminded me of the Weaver when I closed my eyes and imagined him holding me in his strong arms, rocking me to sleep.

Gods, I was delusional, if not doomed. After what he had said to me before the sun rose, I had done exactly what he asked of me before being interrupted by Elowen. I had touched myself, imagining it to be the Weavers hands that pinched the nipples of my breasts, that it was he who fucked my clit with his long fingers before making me find release.

I am doomed.

The smell of sandalwood mingled in the air along with spiced cinnamon, vanilla, and a hint of patchouli, which gave off an exotic, mysterious depth as the scents mingled on my skin and all around me.

I was glad to have cleaned up the blood sprinkled on my freckled face and to have been given the chance to change into new clothes. I truly would have been fine with a blouse and leggings, even if it wouldn't have been appropriate for court.

It would have made me more comfortable to look like my station, and not that of high-born standing. I was a sheep among wolves, and they were slowly closing in on their attack once I gave them the one thing they wanted.

Gold.

"Onyria?" Elowen called from behind me. The girl was a year or so younger than me and was beautiful with her wavy chestnut brown hair that ended at her shoulders. She had rich brown eyes that reminded me of the sweetest chocolate the baker in Cinder Hollow used to make.

I frowned then. Were the baker and his daughter dead? Were their souls tainted as well. I wonder if the Weaver took great pleasure in cutting them down?

No, the baker and his daughter had been kind to me growing up and were one of the only families in Cinder Hollow that didn't believe what the others said about me.

By the gods, I would avenge the innocents that were slaughtered because of the mayor's greed, and for the Weavers satisfaction in the misery of others.

"Onyria, were you listening?" Elowen stood in front of me now, holding gowns up for me to inspect. "Blue or gold?"

I eyed the gowns up and down, taking in how different they were. The gold gown, while enticing, revealed too much and left nothing to the imagination with the slit and the very low neckline, not to mention it was peppered with diamonds and was practically see-through.

"I'll go with the blue one," I said after a long moment of silence. It was due to my not knowing what to say to the maid and what not to say.

For all I knew, she was a spy for the king, and I couldn't afford to make friends and say the wrong things that could lead to my execution. Shaking off the fears of death and betrayal, I smiled when Elowen sauntered over to put the gold gown in a trunk and waved me over to put the blue gown on.

While the gold gown was revealing and shamelessly scandalous, the gown of my choosing was of finer, soft wool in a muted shade of sea blue that reminded me of the flowers in the enchanted forest that only sprouted during the winter season. While Elowen helped tighten the gown, I took in how more refined it was from the gown I had grown accustomed to wearing every day for the last year. The fabric of the blue gown was lightweight, making it seamlessly cozy and comfortable.

The bodice was fitted and laced at the back in bows, thanks to Elowen, with intricate lace trimming along the square neckline and the edges of the sleeves. Playing with the sleeves of the gown, I took in how long they were and how they slightly flared at the cuffs, which, to Elowen, *"adds a touch of elegance to lure the king's eye."*

That was the other thing that had me on edge, and kept the hairs behind my neck erect. Everyone in the castle knew of the king's curse and what my supposed claim meant for him if I could provide him with golden straws.

I am going to die.

I pinched my brows and ignored that thought, so I could focus on what Elowen was asking me to do now. It took me three strides across the room to get used to the full skirt that flew smoothly to the ground, with a slight train at the back that I kept tripping over. By the time I did it, she pulled me to the vanity; she said the king wished to present it to me.

Unsurprisingly, it is gold.

"You look like the emblem of royalty; if only you'd allow me to pierce your ears so I could hook these diamond earrings to them and maybe you could wear a necklace," Elowen rambled, but I shook my head.

I didn't want to feel like more of an imposter than I already was. Not when so many in Anduin could only ever dream of such a feat happening to them in this lifetime.

"I like it this way," I replied. "If it helps, I will wear that ring." I pointed to the ring in question, and Elowen beamed with such glee; her joy's light could have rivaled that of the sun.

The ring was gold with a dark blue stone in the center and was circled by smaller diamonds. I wasn't sure why, but it reminded me of a similar ring I had seen somewhere; I just couldn't place where, and most importantly, why?

"Thank the stars," Elowen said as she slipped the ring onto my finger. Grabbing a comb from the vanity, she then quickly started brushing through my auburn hair that cascaded in rich, radiant waves, each strand a melodious blend of deep red and rich earthy brown. From the reflection in the vanity mirror, the sun danced upon it, divulging a range of mellow tones that transferred from a dark, velvety chestnut to rufescent highlights.

Elowen hummed a tune while meticulously braiding my hair, leaving a few strands loose to frame my face. "What is that song you are humming?" I asked to kill the quiet that had settled between us.

"It's a lullaby my mother used to sing to me before I went to bed, my lady," she explained, and I could have sworn I felt sorrow lacing her words, which pinched my heart.

"What happened to her?" I pushed, not sure why I wanted to know, especially since I hated when people brought up my mother.

I looked up then and caught Elowen's tearful gaze in the mirror before she tried to whip it away when I turned to face her.

"I am sorry; you do not need to tell me if it hurts you to relieve such memories," I said, and it was the truth because I knew what that kind of pain felt like; the aching in one's heart was a growing hole that would never fill completely.

"No, no, it is alright," Elowen assured me as she sniffled. "My mother was a beautiful lady of the court, so graceful in the way she held herself that it caught the eye of the previous king."

Knots formed in the pit of my stomach as I knew where this had gone. I took Elowen's hands in my own and gave them a squeeze for encouragement to either keep going, or stop here. I wouldn't blame her if she did not wish to share the rest of her story with me.

"The king, so in love, invited her to dine with him on most occasions, but she refused him at every turn, until one day." Elowen bowed her head, her chestnut brown hair hiding her face momentarily, before she gathered herself. "He came to her home, and—" the maid broke into sobs, and I quickly shot to my feet and wrapped her in my arms.

I knew the royal family were a bunch of monsters that coveted beauty above all, but to chase after one who had it and only assault her was vile.

Fury burned in the core of my body, and only one thought fueled my next words: "Is the old king still alive?"

Elowen nodded, and her cries grew more violent as her body shook in my arms. "I am the bastard daughter of the High King of Valtain and sister to the king of the gold palace and three rivers of Anduin."

Everything in me froze as if ice had filled my lungs, taming the fiery fury that had risen in my soul. The High King of Valtain was Midas' father, and Elowen's? I didn't want to call on the Weaver, but for Elowen, I would. Her mother deserved justice for the wrong committed against her, and I would make sure of it.

I held Elowen tighter in my embrace as her cries turned into shallow breathing before she broke the hug and straightened herself.

"Why do you work as a maid for King Midas if he is your brother?" I asked. "Though you are a—" I didn't like the word; it tasted sour and rotten on my tongue. "A product of the old king's vileness, you should still have a say in what you do, where, and how you live."

Elowen nodded. "I do, and I chose this," she said before continuing. "Don't let *Rhydian's* cold demeanor get to you, Onyria, for he can be kind, fair, and a just king when given the chance."

My eyes widened at the use of the king's true name. "You call him Rhydian?" I said, it was more for me than a question for her.

How many others used his name so freely? Was it only when he wasn't around to exact punishment for uttering his given name?

"I do; those he considers family or friends call him Rhydian," Elowen confirmed for me as she hooked an arm with me and directed us towards the door.

So, this was it.

I would finally leave this chamber, and if all went well, I could ask for my freedom since I was sure the king did not want a commoner as his pattern, his equal—his queen.

"What do his enemies call him?" I asked when we strode through the halls of the golden palace. Maids and knights alike bowed upon seeing Elowen, and some even glanced at me and gave me a smile.

Was it for encouragement for what I was about to face?

I couldn't be certain, but I was certain of one thing: The people in the castle knew of Elowen's relations to the king, and treated her as royalty when she walked among them.

Maybe she was being truthful, and Midas did have a kind heart if he allowed his people to show his sister the respect she deserved.

Not that bastard children received such kindness in other kingdoms, from what I heard from vendors who passed through Cinder Hollow.

I wasn't in my hometown anymore.

The only sound other than my rapid breathing that could be heard was that of my heels as they clicked against the golden floor of the hall, as we strode straight for two tall, gilded doors.

My heart sped in pace as the doors were opened by the knights stationed there to guard the dining hall. Elowen let go of me then and said something to the guard to my left in such a low tone that I could not hear what they were saying.

Elowen looked confused but hid her expression behind a wall of a false smile as she patted my shoulders and whispered into my ear, "Rhydian isn't playing by the rules, Onyria; he's dismissed court and will be the only one to see you now."

"What does this mean?" I asked.

Elowen smiled. "Don't be afraid to show him your fangs and claws, my lady, and you just might survive the first round." She bowed and excused herself from my side before I could ask her the meaning behind her words.

I didn't look back as she left me standing there in front of the open doors like a blind fool, facing my fate alone. I took a deep breath, taking one step before the other as I walked into the sunlit room to face King Rhydian Midas.

Chapter 6

Onyria

The King sat at the head of the mahogany table, which was full of desserts and fruits. Cakes with purple and green frosting were as high as the oval mirror in my room, towering before me.

The chandeliers overhead twinkled with the light of the sun, but my gaze seemed to always find the king, as he was only watching me with those brown eyes that roared with flames in them.

Gone was the crown he wore when we first met, leaving his golden locks to fall forward above his brow. He wore a dark blue tunic with a gold chainmail vest over it. Behind him was a black cloak with a gilded lion broach, draped over the mighty golden chair he sat on.

"Good morrow, lady Blackwood," Midas said with a cunning smile on his face. "I believe you have something for me."

At the mention of the golden straw he wished for me to present to him, I pulled out the golden straw I had placed on the sleeve of my gown.

I strode towards him slowly, counting each breath I took as I felt the sinking feeling that I was making a mistake by giving him this straw. When I finally reached him, Midas stood, and our chests nearly brushed against one another.

"Well?" he mused, an eyebrow rising when I held out the golden straw that wrapped around my finger like silk for him.

"Does this meet your satisfaction, my king?" I asked, and I remembered what Elowen had said about not speaking unless Midas gave me permission, but I was done following the rules as well.

No one would tell me what to do any longer, and not even this king would determine what would be done with my life.

I refused to think he would think of marriage as both a reward and a way for him to be rid of his golden touch. I had noticed the leather gloves he wore when he took the golden straw into his hands.

There would be only one way I could prove I wasn't Midas' savior, and that would be to touch his skin.

I would turn to gold, but I was sure the Weaver could undo it; he could free me so that our bargain stayed intact.

Without hesitating, I raised a hand to Midas' cheek, but like the strike of lightning, he grabbed my wrist with his gloved hand.

"What do you think you are doing?" he demanded, his fiery gaze burning holes into my green eyes that trailed to his lips.

"Please don't kill me," I pleaded.

Midas' smile that he had plastered on his lips faltered. "What?"

Gods, I blamed the Weaver for turning me into a sinner, and before Midas could stop me, I pressed our chests together and stood tall on my toes as I kissed him.

It was more like a peck from my end as Midas simply stood there, dropping my wrist from his grasp, but then the air in the room shifted and his hands were on my waist.

The kiss started sweet and became desperate as Midas devoured me and yearned for only me as our tongues and teeth clashed in an uncontrollable frenzy that neither one of us wanted to end. As if realizing what he'd done, the king pulled away from me with a sinister laugh that echoed in the dining hall, reverberating off the walls.

"Gods, the fates are cruel," he eyed me as I backed away from him, he took a step towards me with seemingly confident strides.

I wasn't sure what I was doing, but I wanted this. I wanted him; every soul-crushing tether told me this was right, and by the look on his face, so was he.

His rich brown eyes glowed a fiery gold as he caught my waist in his grasp and pulled me closer to him until all I could smell was a vigorous blend of vetiver, leather, cedarwood, the fresh sophistication touch of bergamot, something musky, and a slight hint of cloves.

"Tell me this isn't what you wanted," Midas said. Gone was the cold in his eyes that no longer burned like a thousand comets all set to burn me.

No longer were thoughts or fears of what the Weaver planned to do to me plaguing me in this moment, just that of the king and what I wanted.

What do I want?

I wasn't sure, but maybe Midas was the answer to the burning question. Though this could be a lustful feeling due to the fact that he could safely touch me, I wasn't entirely frightened of him killing me after I gave him my heart.

But Midas could order for my heart to be carved out of my body and given to him to be immortalized in gold. Both men were dangerous, and I couldn't afford to fall for either of them.

Gods, they made it so hard not to look at them and not want to bend to their will. "I don't think I can," I confessed to him in a weak whisper.

Midas smiled, leaning in and breathing in my scent. "You have all the power, Songbird, and please," he paused. "Call him Rhydian."

My head was spinning, or maybe that was the world around me. Was this going too fast, or was that just my heart threatening to break my rib cage?

"Why are you doing this?" I asked. "You wanted me dead when we met; I am a commoner; you don't even know me, and I..."

I froze at that last one, my eyes searching for any hint that Midas, no, Rhydian, was playing some game to trap me.

I couldn't spin straw into gold, but I could touch him, and he could touch me without turning me into a gilded statue. Gods, the fates truly were cruel for dealing me such a terrible hand.

Prophecy or not, I wasn't the one for Midas, and he wasn't mine. We would only disappoint each other until he killed me for learning all the lies told to him.

Not to mention, I was a fraud who would be gaining a crown and a throne that I didn't deserve. Maybe this was what the Weaver wanted to happen once I presented the golden straw to Rhydian.

The Weaver wanted the king's riches, or something only I could give Rhydian, but what? What did the Weaver want from a mortal king when he had magic at his fingertips?

I watched as Rhydian removed his gloves with ease before placing them on the table beside us. I flinched when the knuckles of his fingers brushed against my cheek as he asked, "What were you going to say?"

"I—"

If I told him, would he understand, or would he have me hanged for deceiving him and playing along with my father's lie? I wouldn't; I didn't deserve his forgiveness, let alone mine.

I should have come clean the moment I handed him the straw when I had the chance. But then, would I have challenged the extent of the prophecy?

"Can I tell you a secret, my little Songbird?" Rhydian asked.

Words failed me as I opened my mouth and then closed it. I couldn't be certain I wouldn't blurt out the truth in my moment of weakness.

I nodded my answer when I saw Rhydian looking at me, as if I were the key to a long-forgotten question. But eyes could deceive just as words and actions could as well.

The air shifted again, and a golden dome swirled around us. My eyes widened as I reached out to touch it. "What is the meaning of this?" I asked in awe.

"Centuries ago, I helped a sorceress, and in thanks, she granted me one wish," Rhydian explained. Somehow my mind wasn't fazed by the news that Rhydian was hundreds of years old, but that I felt as though I knew this story.

"What did you wish for?" I inquired, but I knew what he wished for; I saw it swirling all around us as we spoke so closely to one another.

Rhydian's smile grew as if amused by my question, as though he knew I was merely asking to get air in my lungs.

"In exchange for safety, I wished for everything I touched to turn to gold, my clever Songbird," he confirmed, even though we both knew it. Blood ran cold in my body as I saw Rhydian's gaze, which shifted from kind and warm to cold and sinister. "But along with her eternal gift, she gave me a prophecy and a warning that the one my heart would belong to would deceive me with lies and deceit."

I knew I wasn't the one he spoke of, but that didn't stop me from shaking my head. "I can explain," I stuttered.

"Yes, you will, or your head will roll, love," he warned.

I swallowed hard, playing with the hem of my gown as I whipped my hands out of the sweat that was gathered on my palms. "The night you locked me in the tower," I closed my eyes and prayed to the gods and to the universe to spare me. "A creature known as the Weaver came to me and promised me whatever I desired in exchange for the thing I valued most."

"Let me guess; that's me." Rhydian said, his voice and tone venomous like the snakes in the mountains of Anduin. The kings stepped forward as I backed away before slamming into a wall. I found my body trapped between a gold wall and the king, which I was sure caused it to be so solid.

I laughed. "Not everything is about you."

Rhydian smirked and pressed into me. He held my chin up between his fingers, our lips nearly grazing. "Lay with me, and you'll see everything will be about me, my cock, my riches, and my seat of power over the realm."

I wasn't sure if he was paying attention when I first arrived in the dining hall, but the first thing I did was grab a knife off the table. After my encounter with the Weaver and stabbing him, he'd taken my last weapon and threw it out the window.

I wouldn't be so foolish this time. Gold made Rhydian immortal, but it didn't make him invulnerable to death. I held the knife low to his trousers, and when the pointed end tip touched him, he flinched slightly.

Rhydian looked down, and in that moment, two expressions crossed his face as his brows rose in shock, and what I could only assume was him being impressed that I would ever draw a weapon on a royal.

"Do anything to me, and I will make sure you never lay with anyone," I hissed.

Rhydian chuckled and didn't make a move to grab the knife from me. "Territorial, are we?"

"Hardly."

"Shall we test that theory?" He challenged.

I arched a brow. "This means nothing," I said assuringly as I brought the knife up from his balls to his throat.

"Agreed," he replied, mischief glinting in his eyes. "But first, what did the Weaver do for you?"

I smiled and eyed the golden straw wrapped around his finger. "The one thing you wanted from me," I confessed, and Rhydian's smile grew.

"You are a deceiver of men, *Onyria*," he purred, and my name sounded like pure sin coming out of his mouth.

I laughed. "And you are a vile man that locks women in cages for your own greed," I shot back, but I found that I was no longer mad because it brought me to this moment, so close to him, to smell him and touch him.

Gods, I might actually like him.

"I want to be free of it, Songbird, of the gold, of the magic," he confessed, and with a snap of his finger, the dome around us dissolved and a gold rose appeared in his hand. "I want to smell roses without fear of turning them into gold, I want to embrace my sister without watching her stand still like a fucking gold statue." Rhydian stepped closer to me, brushing a strand of my hair behind my ear. "I want to be happy with someone who doesn't just see me for the safety I can provide them but for the life and love I wish to share with them. If I have to do vile things to achieve it, then so be it, and if it makes me a villain, then I would gladly do it again, and you want to know why?"

I nodded, too stunned to speak, but what could I say when Rhydian stood so close? His presence put me in a frenzy. I wasn't sure how, or if, I wanted to escape.

The knife I held to his throat pressed harder into his skin until a pebble of his blood leaked down the blade. I went to pull it away, but Rhydian stopped me, and that's when I noticed the color of his blood.

It's gold.

"I can't die, love; I've tried; I have tasted every poison known to man; I have chased every whisper of a weapon that could kill an immortal," he sighed. "I've slit my own throat too many times to count, gone to war, and come back bathed in the blood of those that couldn't defeat me. I've met every known powerful witch across the continent and beyond, and I've failed a thousand times to end this miserable existence, but I find myself here and with you now, the answer to my problem, and I no longer want this life to end," Rhydian confessed.

"I am not the answer to your problems, Rhydian," I said.

"But you could be," he replied. The world stopped spinning as I watched in utter silence as Rhydian dropped to one knee, and with a flick of his wrist, a golden box appeared in his hand. "Will you marry me, Onyria Blackwood of Cinder Hollow, and help me break my curse so we may have the life I wish to show you?"

Chapter 7

Onyria

Everything in my bones said yes, but something in my gut told me the Weaver was one step closer to getting what he wanted. I slipped out of Rhydian's hold and shook my head.

"I can't, no, I shouldn't; you don't know me; you locked me away without food, and then you ambush me now with this?" I was rambling now. "Why do you get to have your happy ending, but I am left to just sit by and accept what is given to me? Why don't I get what I want?"

My vision blurred, and tears streaked my face, I wrapped my arms around myself for support. I wasn't sure why I told Rhydian all that I did; it didn't matter; the fates wanted me to marry him. The Weaver more than pushed me into Rhydian's arms by helping me.

Rhydian dropped his hands then, and the box turned to gold dust. "What do you want, Onyria?"

"My freedom!" I snapped.

Was it so hard to believe that not everyone would willingly accept a crown? Not to mention heirs would be expected of me, and I would have to wear more gowns, attend court, and be someone I wasn't.

"I see," Rhydian said. He threw his head back before meeting my blurred gaze. "I'll tell you what, Songbird. If you help me break my curse, I will set you free."

My heart sank at his words, but my soul screamed in thanks that he was willingly letting me go, *but only if I helped him.*

"Doesn't that mean I would have to marry you?" I asked.

Rhydian shook his head. "True love's kiss should break my gilded chains."

I broke into a fit of laughter. Surely this was a jest, if not a ploy, to trap me into falling for him like some love-sick puppy dog.

I wouldn't allow it.

"Are you afraid of falling for me?" Rhydian asked.

I crossed my arms. "No." I said it too fast for my liking, and we both knew it. The way he watched me should have been sin, so pleading, so much yearning to touch someone who was seemingly immune to his gold touch.

I shouldn't cross the line.

This thing between us wasn't love; it was lust, and one kiss wouldn't help him. If anything, it would disappoint him and make him more than desire to see my head on a pike.

Rhydian pressed himself further against my back, and I caught familiar and new scents wafting from him. A hint of roses, the sweetest presence of light rain during spring—something musky, primal, and raw energy filled my nostrils and leaked from my pores.

Something about him was familiar, but I couldn't shake the feeling that it was something I should not remember, or else the consequences could be dire.

"Are you lying to me?" he asked.

I shook my head. I did not trust myself to say what I should to him anymore; I trusted him to tell me the truth about why we were here.

"What do you want from me this time?" I breathed, and I didn't mean for my words to sound so sensual.

I could feel his wicked smile on my throat as his nose drifted up my neck. There was no doubt in my mind that he was taking in my scent. Part of me wanted to know what he smelled and wondered if he would trail kisses next as he took complete control.

"How about you give me a kiss, little *Drithalis*, before I allow you to ease the ache you give me?" he said, his fingers tracing a line down my spine and causing me to shiver.

That word again. *Drithalis*. Oh gods, no, no, no.

I turned to face Rhydian, and my heart sank to new lows I didn't think possible. Gone were the brown eyes to reveal icy blue eyes rimmed with gold; his skin wasn't pale any longer and was a warmer tone kissed by the sun; and his golden blonde hair was now mixed into hair as dark as night, until the only gold in his hair were highlights in the sea of obsidian.

The Weaver and the king stood before me as one person, and when I opened my mouth to scream, to shove the knife I held in my hand into his heart, gold and black tendrils swirled around me, locking me in place and covering my mouth as I dropped the knife from my hand.

"Did you think escaping me would be so easy, foolish mortal?" The Weaver asked. Or was it Midas or Rhydian? I watched as he undid the buttons of his coat and threw it like it was trash to be forgotten.

"You asked me what I wanted," I stuttered, fear gripping at my bones like talons to see the monster before me in such a way.

"You can beg, run, and even try to hide from me, *Drithalis*, but know this," he leaned in, slowly turning me around to face outside the gilded arch window we stood in front of as he whispered, "I will hunt you down to the ends of the earth and make sure you know who you belong to."

"I—" What did it all mean? I wanted to ask, but my brain was muddled and left shattered by the wake of his near presence and his crushing words.

He has been here the entire time. He was the demon the Fae feared, the Weaver, the king of Anduin, and my captive. Gods, did my father know? Did Elowen, the servants, and the guards in this fucking castle know?

"Fuck you!" was all I managed.

I felt his smirk on my earlobe as my body betrayed me. I arched into him slightly as he turned me back to face him before trapping me against his body and his magic. I could almost make out the marked skin underneath his now-midnight tunic, with unending swirls and dialects I couldn't decipher.

I gasped upon feeling the light press of the closed window against my back now, as he whispered, "You will, Onyria, very soon."

A moan escaped my lips upon feeling his cock press against me. Gods, it must be large for it to be settled so nicely between my legs. I couldn't help grinding against him for more friction between us, and I smiled mischievously when a guttural sound vibrated from his chest.

This is wrong.

But no longer would I let this male have control over me and what I desired. If he wanted to play this game, then I would play harder to win.

He was the God of deceivers; his magic was his mask, and he played so many roles so he could win. But I would make him wish he had lost when he had the chance.

"You tricked me." I bit my bottom lip as he wrapped a hand around my throat, applying the sweetest amount of pressure. "Why? I should hate you, but I can't find it in my heart either."

It was the sickening truth I tried to ignore. He was a monster, a liar, and I should loathe him more than I do my own father, who betrayed me, but I couldn't find it in me either.

"Life is so much more fun when you are playing a game, but to answer your question," he rubbed his thumb along my jaw and forced me to look at him. "I needed you to see me as I am and understand that I am cruel, but I have a heart. I did not slaughter your town, but I did kill the mayor. Unfortunately, the same cannot be said about your sheriff, though."

Leave it to that fucking bastard to escape the most ruthless man alive and the king of our own kingdom. Wherever Thadeus found himself now, I hoped he would rot in hell, or else I would hunt him down myself.

Until then, I already had one monster to deal with, and I wasn't sure if I wanted to kill him with my bare hands as much as I wanted the taste of his lips on mine.

"But why?"

The Weaver sighed. "You will understand one day when the fog on your mind lifts."

The fog on my what?

I gritted my teeth and pulled away from him. Was everything a game for him to muse over, even when he knew he'd win? Why must I be left in the dark, while he knows what is to come?

My head was fuming as I shoved him. "You knew I couldn't spin your stupid straw into gold, and you still had me come in here like a nervous fool." I pushed against him harder as tears stung the back of my eyes. "You told me the poor story of Midas only for you to reveal you are him and he is you; you played me for a fool. Why?"

"Because Onyria, life is cruel; the world we live in is not kind; it does not care for heroes or villains, not even if your souls are pure, for it is full of people meant to break you so you may rise or fall," he explained, but it made no sense; it was the words of a mad lunatic at best. "I couldn't be honest with you because I couldn't be certain I could trust you; you were prophesied to either usher in a new era alongside me or doom me and my people."

"I never asked for any of this!" I shouted.

He threw his head back and laughed dryly as he grabbed hold of my neck. "Admit it, you liked this, didn't you? The lies, the sneaking around, the plotting and scheming," he asked, and before I could answer, he pressed harder into me, and

I whimpered. I needed more friction; I wanted more, even though I was furious with him to the point where my brain might combust. "You like my hands around that delicate throat of yours, don't you? You enjoyed the games and everything that came with them. Confess."

"You're sick," I hissed against gritted teeth. I knew it wasn't an answer either and relished the fact that it annoyed him to no end.

When he applied more pressure, I nodded. Okay, maybe I was losing a bit of control; I found it hard not to like the things he did to me when it was the most dangerous, reckless kind of adventure away from home I'd ever get in this life; it was driving me mad like the Hatter from that story my mother used to read to me as a child.

It is exciting to live on the deep end.

Gods, I wanted the feel of this male all over me, around me, and in me, and I wouldn't deny it any longer. When he least expected it, I grabbed his straining cock. The outline of it wasn't hard to see in his trousers, and I could almost make out the size of it.

Gods. That was not going to fit inside me, let alone in my mouth.

"Don't worry, love," he said assuringly. "I will make sure you take every last inch of me like a *good girl*." I was suddenly aware of the distance between us as he collected his coat off the floor, where he had discarded it. "But first, if you want my cock, *Drithalis*, you will have to earn it, and before that can happen, I need you ready in my chambers in an hour before I hunt you down and fuck you like some wild animal in the middle of a rut."

I glared at him. "Excuse me?"

My sinister demon laughed, and it brought a thundering thrill to my beating heart that raced against the speed of my thoughts.

Rhydian leaned in and whispered, "You will run, and I will chase. If you lose, I choose where and how I will fuck you. If you win, I will still fuck you, but you get to decide how I fuck you first."

"That doesn't sound fair or a win-win scenario," I pointed out, and it earned me another laugh I hadn't realized I'd grown accustomed to hearing like a soothing melody in the wind.

Rhydian lightly bit my earlobe before saying, "Trust me when I say that this is as fair as I will ever be with you, *Valea'mara*."

Chapter 8

Onyria

The castle was like a maze meant to confuse me by the time I reached the grand steps. Guards bowed upon seeing me, and I barely had time to take in their clad gold armor.

I noticed then that they also wore white cloaks to signify their loyalty to the royal family and to their oaths sworn to the king.

The faster I sprinted up the stairs and through hallways of gold walls with intricate detailing, lion trimmings, and walls decorated with tapestries of the old and new gods of our realm.

One could learn all they needed to know from my shadow just by gazing at the gods he recognized and the wars he chose to represent in the art that decorated his walls. I stopped for a moment to catch my breath when I noticed the banner in front of me.

King Rhydian Midas was a part of House Dragoth, and their colors were red and black, but everywhere I looked, I only found his colors, white and gold.

Was the king not close with his father, the High King? Maybe it wasn't my place, but something had shifted between us; his wall came down a bit, and he was letting me in.

That was a good thing, something I could use for when I needed to escape this place, but for now I would enjoy this beautiful—Oh gods, was it already the afternoon? We had been so distracted conversing that I hadn't had breakfast.

Damnit.

I needed to keep up my strength, and I couldn't do that on an empty stomach. If I turned back now, would he even know? Rhydian said he'd hunt me down, but he couldn't do that if he couldn't find me.

A scream lodged deep in my throat when a hand came for my shoulder. I quickly turned on my heel to find Elowen; her eyes widened when she saw I was prepared to punch her. Embarrassed by my actions, I felt my cheeks heat as I dropped my fist, curtsied, and then rose to smile at her.

"What are you doing here, Onyria?" Elowen asked.

Was she shocked to find me still alive or confused that I was out of breath and taking in the one banner of their family crest of a dragon being impaled by a sword?

"I am running from your brother; what does it look like to you?" I shot back, bending down before bracing my hands on my knees for support as I greedily took in a lungful of air.

"Oh, I see," was all Elowen said. "Well, might I suggest something to you?" Raising a brow, I leaned against the wall behind me and nodded.

"Take those stairs," she said, pointing her ruby-painted finger to an arched entryway that led to spiraling stairs. "On your first left, you'll find crimson doors; hide there and you'll surely win," she winked and sauntered away.

I couldn't tell if she was truly helping me or if she somehow knew what Rhydian was getting at, so she figured she'd help him along. By the gods, could anyone in this castle be trusted, or was I doomed to always be trapped in a game where I had no idea what the rules were?

Deciding that Elowen's suggested path was the only one I had, or better yet, the only one my mind could think of, I dashed for the spiraling stairs.

It was odd how, the deeper I went into the castle, the less gold I saw. From the stairs to the walls, everything I heard was cobblestone, even the lion statues, which were representations of Midas' sigil.

All his guards had a lion on the breastplates of their armor and on the back of their cloaks. It was as if he purposely differentiated himself from his father so he could be seen as his own man.

It made sense and was understandable. No child wanted to live in the shadows of their parents for the rest of their lives, but the fact that Rhydian only had one banner in this entire castle that told the origin of his story was odd.

I cast the thoughts out of my mind as I reached the final step before stepping into the dimly lit hall, and upon turning left, I saw the deep crimson doors.

They were high and reached the ceiling like the rest of the doors in the castle, but I realized that these doors were made of bloodstone.

Interesting.

What else was Rhydian doing with bloodstone, and why was it primarily used to make these doors? Upon better inspection, I realized dark roots grew along the sides of the door and made an intricate design of swirls all over the entrance of my destination.

I glanced behind me before taking a deep breath and pushing open the door. My nose met stale air and dust particles as I entered the large chambers.

Everywhere the eye could see, furniture was covered, cobwebs inhabiting the corners of the ceilings, and spiders the size of my fist crawled into the shadows.

The further I explored, the more I saw, and the more I got the sense that these chambers had been abandoned for some time.

But I stopped dead in my tracks upon noticing the silky red dress hung by the fireplace. If this was some kind of ploy by Elowen to get her brother to lose his mind, then I had to thank her.

He was going to either kill me for even letting the thought of putting something so revealing on me or thank me before he tore it off my body.

Deciding it'd be the latter, I made quick work of my blue gown and undid the lace on the square neckline before fumbling to undo the lace on my back. When nothing but my undergarments remained, I pondered if it made sense to keep them on with the nearly see-through red silk.

Was I seriously considering standing here naked for a man?
Yes.

But also, no, this wasn't just for Rhydian. Putting on this scandalous piece of fabric was for me to also redefine the boundaries of what was comfortable for me and what wasn't. Now was the best time to test the waters and decide whether or not I could live in my Shadows world, and still be me.

This dress wouldn't change that.

It took some time, but I managed to get the silky see-through dress on. My back was bare to the crisp air around me, and my breasts were nearly out but covered by thin strings of lace that stopped above my waist. My hands roamed the curves of my body and took in how perfectly the dress fit, as though it were made for me.

A tingling sensation coursed through my entire being and lit a spark in my body, and when my eyes landed on him, I assumed then that these were his chambers.

"Does this mean I won?"

Never in my life had I felt temptation lure me to the darkest pits of desire, but I wanted him like I needed air, and gods be damned if I didn't have him at least once.

"No," he replied.

My weaver didn't say anything else as I approached him like a predatory feline. When I reached him, I slowly rose on my toes and whispered into his ear, "Then what are you waiting for, *Weaver*? Claim me like I am yours so that I may never forget who owns me."

He had me in a chokehold then and slammed my body against the wall beside the now-roaring fireplace with ferocity I hadn't expected from him but knew I should have when a burning sensation like liquid fire thrilled my body with anticipation, all the way down to my clit.

He chuckled then. "You are right to believe you are mine; your life belongs to me, along with your soul and this body." His hands trailed down from my spine to my navel until he reached my waist. He paused there before continuing lower until he reached for the ends of my dress and tore it down the middle, like it was merely paper to him. He growled upon noticing how truly bare I was for him, and I enjoyed every moment of it.

"Where is the rest of this gown?" He asked.

"You're holding it," I said, eyeing the red silk fabric of the dress I had just put on moments before he arrived.

"I hope you didn't think you could keep such a thing," he mused as he threw the rest of the dress to the ground, his eyes traveling over my body hungrily.

Everything was visible to him, and I didn't dare cower from him as his eyes roamed over my plump breasts, stomach, waist, and lower to my aching core. I knew was already wet for him.

He was like a man starving for his last meal, and I devoured every ounce of it as his featherlight touch grazed my bare skin. His need and utter desire for me to submit to him were written all over his roaming gaze, which said one thing.

I wasn't leaving these chambers tonight.

The Weaver snapped his fingers then, and a settee appeared with golden plush pillows before he sat. I watched as he used his magic so freely with a flick of his wrist, but I hadn't realized when a mini table appeared for him with a glass full of crimson wine.

I arched a brow at him when his attention was no longer on me, and when he noticed, my Shadow smirked and tilted his head back as he took a swig of his wine.

"What's the matter, *Drithalis*? Not willing to let a man prepare himself before he has his breakfast or, better yet, brunch?" He asked with an amused look when I stared at him in utter confusion.

He had no food set up in front of him. Just the tanker of wine, his glass, the now empty table behind us, and a bowl of grapes in his hand. But he watched me and drank me in, like the sweetest cherry wine. My knees buckled at the vivid thoughts that played through my mind, and my eyes widened then as I finally took in his meaning.

I had caught him off guard with the new dress that didn't need undergarments, and now he was changing his prize.

The Weavers smile became devilish as a knowing look slipped between us. "What else do you desire, other than a kiss?" I asked, taking slow steps toward him.

His fangs were on full display as he bit his lower lip, eyeing me with those icy orbs of his that seemed to *warm* my blood and my determination to have him.

"On your knees, Songbird," he ordered, and I obliged.

When I reached for the buttons of his breeches, he stopped me, holding my wrist away from him as he leaned forward. "Naughty girls don't get to be in control, *Drithalis*," he purred.

"Then punish me." I breathed, not caring how far or how wrong this should feel when, in the end, it just felt right.

The Weaver—

"You may call me Rhydian from now on; only those meant to fear me call me the Weaver or Midas, but you can call me Rhydian," he said, cutting off my train of thought. "And know that when you gag my name with your rosy lips around my cock as I fuck your mouth, that you are being punished by your God."

Shadows and gold swirled around us, and my hands were bound behind my bare back. His shadows had undressed me completely, the last of the torn fabrics falling to my knees, but what caught my gaze was truly mouth-watering.

The Weaver—Rhydian—leaned back on the settee in all his naked glory, his cock standing thick and erect like the tower we had begun this game in. How was that supposed to fit in my throat, let alone my core?

"I told you before, every last inch of me will fit, and you will take it like a good girl," Rhydian said. I had almost forgotten he could hear my thoughts when he reminded me of his earlier words.

Arousal leaked from my center and trailed down my thighs, as I stared shamelessly at his massive erection.

My hands were still bound behind my back, and when I leaned forward to lick him and taste the precum that had begun to bubble at the tip, his magic lifted me in the air until I settled on top of him.

My clit rubbed against his cock, but I was taken away from any friction as I went higher until my arousal trailed liquid fire on his bare muscular chest. I was so high above him that his lips were pressing on my center.

"Oh gods," I whimpered. He planned on devouring me.

The realization that I had been correct in my assumption ran through me until I was begging to touch him and for him to touch me.

"There's only one God that is willing to hear you, love, and he's about to eat," he teased. His breath blew a cold breeze against my clit and I was writhing against his gold shadows for him to finally lick me, ease the ache, and put me out of my misery.

"What do you say, Onyria? Shall I grant us our wish today or later tonight when the rest of the castle sleeps?"

I didn't care who heard us if that was what he meant; I needed him now before the fire burning inside of me became a raging inferno. "Please, Rhydian," I begged. "I'll do anything you ask of me."

I didn't care that words were important when it came to him and could be a trap. My name coming out of his lips was like a collision of dying stars, and I wanted more.

"As you wish, my sweet little *Drithalis*."

His mouth was on me in seconds, and his tongue slowly swirled around my clit before penetrating my center with ease thanks to my arousal. I screamed his name, not caring who heard me as I rocked against his mouth.

I couldn't use my hands, but I'd be damned if I didn't get as much friction out of this as possible.

Nothing was slow with Rhydian once I began to ride his face; he gripped my ass hard, licked the liquid heat from my thighs, and devoured me in a way that was primal and claiming as he nibbled and sucked the arousal out of me like I was his divine drink of the gods, the liquid only they could drink - ambrosia.

When he pulled away, he said, "That's it, Drithalis, fuck my face."

His golden shadows dissipated then. I moaned, and I gripped onto his midnight and gilded hair, rocking back and forth atop his mouth as he licked and sucked away my arousal.

"Yes, yes, yes!" I screamed unashamedly that we could be heard, consequences be damned. "Just like that, don't stop."

He didn't. Rhydian let me ride his mouth until I found my release, and at the feel of hot strings of cum on my back registered in my mind, I realized then so had he.

We lay there on the settee in ethereal silence, my face on his bare chest as he played with my fiery hair. I drew the lines of his tattoos as sleep made its way through my body.

"Onyria?"

"Hmm?" That was all I replied with before looking up to meet his awaiting gaze.

"I'll take that kiss now," he said, and I no longer felt scared to give him a true kiss since he'd already taken or rather given me something much more valuable.

This memory.

I slid up his body until our faces were at eye level as I pressed a hand to his once-ice-cold cheek, which was now as warm as our touching skin.

How had I not realized how cold his skin was before, and how come it is warm now? My face heated at the thought that what we had done had melted away his cold shield. Or had I gotten comfortable with it, and to me, it was warm now that our skins were freely touching without the barrier of clothes?

I shook the thought out of my mind, leaned in, and closed my eyes once our lips met. The kiss was nothing like when he kissed me for the first time in the dining hall or when he pressed light kisses to my thighs or devoured the rest of me. This was slow yet passionate, gentle yet laced with so much yearning that my heart could melt from the magnitude of its magic.

Yes. This kiss was magic as our tongues clashed, and electrifying tingles shot through my body when his magic hummed with the beat of our synced hearts.

"Stay," I pleaded, pressing our foreheads together before our eyes met. His ice-blue eyes searched my green ones, and I knew the answer before he opened his mouth.

"Don't you think I should be the one asking you that?" Rhydian reminded me as he pushed a strand of my auburn hair behind my ear.

Sighing, I nodded. "Then I shall stay, but you must never lie to me, Rhydian, or else I will leave you and never return."

Sadly, betrayal was inevitable, and he taught me that. This world and our lives were cruel, along with the people that lived in them and the gods who governed them. Though none of that meant I couldn't have a little bit more fun until the day came that our souls would crack and splinter from heartbreak or worse...

Rhydian must have heard my thoughts then because he arched a brow at me and said, "Whatever it is you are planning to—"

I pressed a finger to his lips before trailing kisses down from his throat, to his chest, and to his abdomen until I reached what I wanted from him. I gripped his cock in my hands and watched in amusement as Rhydian's head fell back.

"Fuck, Onyria," he cursed underneath his breath.

I smiled against his thigh and gently kissed him there before kissing his shaft and pumping it up and down in a slow rhythm. "You will," I teased.

Rhydian growled, but before he could say anything, I licked his cock from the base to the tip in one languish motion. His entire body seemed to go limp at that very moment, and I was more than pleased to see he wasn't the only one with power when it came to what we wanted.

"Onyria, you don't have to continue if you don't want to..." His words were muffled into a curse or prayer in his language as I took his entire cock into my mouth, gagging upon fitting his entire shaft down my throat.

Gods above, he was a beast.

Rhydian grabbed a fistful of my hair and fucked my face without mercy. I blinked back tears as I grabbed the base of his cock and licked all the way up to the tip once more.

"There will be no other, Rhydian; you belong to me as I am yours," I told him and rose to my feet. He arched a brow at my words, and when I straddled him, he cursed. "Say it."

"Stars, woman, there will be no other for me, as I am yours as you are mine," he replied, his words coming out between curses as I slid my clit over his cock.

Smiling, I grasped his cock in one hand and lined it up with my entrance. There would be no going back after this; our bodies would be joined in more ways than one.

The contract still dangled over my head; pieces of my heart turned into piles of timeless sand only he could pick up, and a dark and wicked part of me didn't care. Sinking his cock into me, I cried out his name as he filled me, and he gripped my ass for support.

"Gods, Rhydian, you're too big," I breathed.

He laughed. "No, love, your body was molded for my cock, so you are going to take every last inch," he said, and with each word, I felt my core clench around him as I took more of him. "Now move your hips, *Valea'mara*."

I did as he asked and rose slightly before slamming back down to meet his wild thrust. "Oh gods!" I screamed.

Rhydian chuckled darkly. "They're not here, love, only me, always just me, your only god," he said, and I had to agree as he fit the last inch of his cock into me.

I clawed at his back before wrapping my arms around his neck and falling into the rhythm of his thrusts, each one wilder than the last.

"That's it, *Valea'mara*, cum all over my cock," Rhydian growled as he nibbled and sucked on my peaked breasts.

"Yes, yes, yes," I screamed, gripping tightly onto his massive shoulders as I chased my own release, and gods, I never wanted this feeling of being filled to end. I felt when our orgasms collided and hot ropes of cum coated my walls, as bliss washed through our entangled bodies.

But all good things must come to an end at some point, and as our orgasms found us and we collapsed against the settee, breathing hard like wild animals covered in sweat, I decided to hells with whatever came next; Rhydian was mine, and we would face whatever came our way together.

Or so I hoped.

Rhydian wrapped his arms around my waist and pulled me in close to his naked body. I felt nothing but warmth radiating off of him.

Suddenly, I heard a rustle of wings, and when I turned to face Rhydian, one dark, feathery wing of pure twilight wrapped around us.

"You have wings," I whispered as I rested my head back on his arm and nuzzled my back further against his chest.

"I was an angel of the gilded legion before I fell into this world, Onyria; now I am something else, dark and corrupted, so don't believe this to be a good omen, for I am still the villain of your story, and I will never be anything else," Rhydian said, his tone laced with sorrow and something else I couldn't place.

I giggled, no longer able to focus on his words. I couldn't help it, not when Rhydian traced the lines on my back, and then my blood stilled from the realization of what he was truly tracing.

My scars.

The mayor and his goons gave me every chance they could when I was caught breaking the laws put in place to keep people like me in line.

"Who gave you these, Onyria?" Rhydian growled.

"I—"

What would he do if I told him? What kind of madness would take over him when he realized he had more than likely killed all of them except for one?

"Onyria," Rhydian hissed, and I realized why. I was all but grinding against his fully erect cock as his hands slipped to my waist. "If you don't tell me who gave you those scars, and stop what you are doing right now," he paused, and I imagined he was swallowing hard as his eyes rolled back from the complete bliss of the promise of connection. "Stars above, woman, I will not be able to restrain myself."

I fully turned to face him, our chests brushing against one another, and his fingers traced swirls along my thigh.

"Rhydian," I said. His name on my lips was like a perfect fantasy dream my mind had conjured to help me cope with the fact that I was a prisoner, but it was a dream that I would waste away in, if it meant I never had to face the outside world. "You aren't the villain of my story."

Though he had said it a while ago and it had nothing to do with the conversation at hand, I needed him to know how much of a savior he was in his own twisted way.

It didn't change the fact that I wanted to escape this place and that I hated him for his lies and his games that led us here on the only settee untouched by dust and cobwebs in these chambers.

Rhydian opened his mouth to speak then. "Don't be so." I held a finger to his lips, enjoying that he closed his eyes when I touched his mouth, as if he liked it too.

"I am not finished," I said. "I have faced many cruel monsters before I met you, and I never once considered you my villain."

It was all I was going to say on the matter of who he was to me and the monsters that inflicted physical pain on me.

Rhydian kissed my fingers before taking my hands in his. "I might not be your villain, *Valea'mara*, but I swear to the old gods and new, I will kill all those who touched you, and I will make sure their deaths are more than double the pain they inflicted on you."

"Why?" I asked, but I knew, and I secretly wanted him to say it to soothe the worry that had built up in the pit of my stomach. The fear that if I closed my eyes, this wonderful dream would end, and that when the sun descended, reality would set in, and I would be sent back to my tower.

"Because *Drithalis*, no one is allowed to touch you and live so long as I live—no one but me," he said, and it came out in a growl.

I felt my cheeks and neck heat as I hid in his chest. "You can't say things like that." I didn't want him to see the extent of what his words did to me, though my thundering heart probably gave me away.

Rhydian held my chin in his fingers, and our eyes locked. The way his icy blue eyes looked into my green ones was like a fairytale of his making; it was a dream that I didn't want to wake from.

He laughed. "I will say whatever I like to my woman," he declared with a kiss that could melt ice and make mountains crumble. It was passionate, slow, and filled with so many meanings I couldn't decipher.

When he pulled away, we were a mess of panting while our eyes searched for one another's unspoken answer. "Rhydian?"

"Yes?"

"What does *Drithalis* mean?"

The smirk on his lips widened into a full smile when he leaned in and whispered into my ear, "It means, *Dreamwalker*, Onyria, because you are the greatest dream to have ever stepped foot in my sleep, and I wish to never wake from them."

My vision was blurred by unshed tears then. "Rhydian—"

His lips were on mine in the next moment, and I melted into him and his hold as he gripped my thigh and brought me closer into him as if to mold our bodies together. He kissed my tears away, licked up my throat, and found my lips in the next devouring kiss.

What a sweet dream this was, indeed.

"Please don't leave me when the sun sets, *Drithalis*," Rhydian pleaded. I wasn't sure where that unspoken fear had come from, but I held his cheek in my palm.

"I won't," I replied, and I kissed him harder and more demandingly as we fought for dominance over one another's mouths. "I will never leave you."

Chapter 9

Aurealina

"Aestra'felanis," a familiar voice called out to her from behind her. She stood in the middle of a field peppered with moon roses, gifts from the lunar queen. "My beloved, come dance with me."

She turned then to face the male she had come to love against the laws put in place to keep them apart for all eternity. She admired his crystal amethyst eyes, raven-colored hair with hints of gold, and his bare chest, which was marked by unending tattoos.

Of all the markings on his skin, she admired the one that stretched along his left arm like webs, but she knew better. The tattoo was a declaration of their love; it was a map and a thousand constellations that only she could decipher.

Aurealina had the same markings on her left arm, but where her lover's tattoo was a bright blue like the darkened sky littered with stars, hers was gold and swirled all along her arm to her fingertips.

Together, the constellations created the ultimate bond and completed the map to a place only she could reach—a place she could take him, far away from the decaying world she protected.

She sighed and fully took him in before taking his extended hand in hers. "There is no reality, no realm, or curse that could ever make me tell you no," she said as the male twirled her into his arms and back out so that only their hands and chests connected.

They stayed like that until the birds in their nests sang their songs, and the roses beneath their feet swayed with the summer breeze.

"Good, because I want to dance with you for eternity. I want our souls to immerse themselves in each other until there is nothing left but us," he whispered into her ear.

With a snap of his fingers, music played softly in the warm wind, and the stars above twinkled more with the use of his magic.

Together, they were unstoppable. Aurealina knew this, and she knew why he wanted to dance. It was the same reason she agreed to meet him in the mortal world against her brother and sister's wishes.

It was no longer safe for Aurealina to be here, and without the protection her sibling's realms gave her, she needed to see the male one last time.

"Nyx and his army march to war at first light, my love," she said. How was she to tell him that she did not plan on being on the battlefield? Her fight was among the heavens, where the nightmare of this world would be once her siblings left her. There was so much that Aurealina wished to tell him, but there wasn't enough time. Her time was up; the fates had granted her one final divination, one final warning. Her sacrifice would ensure the safety of thousands until the time came for—Aurealina felt her siblings call to her in her mind before she could formulate her next words. "There will come a time when you will hate me and wish I'd chosen differently."

"What are you saying?" he asked. "Speak plainly."

It wasn't a demand but rather a plea; Aurealina could sense it through the bond. Once her sacrifice was made, the bond would shatter, and he'd be free of her. He'd know what happened and what had caused her soul to depart from existence, but he'd forgive the nightmare.

He would never go against the one that would strike her down, and that was why she had to face him on her own.

"I love you," she said against his lips, and before he could say anything else, she claimed him in a passionate kiss he wouldn't know was a goodbye until the proof of their bond faded.

She'd see her fallen brother soon enough, but before then, she had to say her final goodbyes to her other siblings that still breathed.

Her sweet, determined, and head-strong sisters, whom she had watched grow into mighty goddesses from afar, would be her hardest challenges as they were all older than her.

Life was cruel to Aurealina, but she wouldn't change her life for the world. She did everything she could so that this day wouldn't come, but the fates had other plans.

Now, she had to say her goodbyes and know those she left behind would never forgive her—not her three sisters or her two remaining brothers, not this beautiful male she wished she could spend eternity with, and certainly not herself.

She had failed.

"Please forgive me," she whispered as she peppered kisses against his lips, and before the male could say anything else, she used her power to return to the heavens, where he couldn't follow.

Tears streaked her face, as his screams for her to return to him pounded through the bond. She closed her eyes as fresh tears flowed freely now that she had materialized in her eldest's sister's throne room.

"I guess this means it's my turn then," her sister, Seraphina, said from atop her glass throne that trapped the true beauty of stars within it.

Aurealina took a deep breath and squared her shoulders as she faced her sister, the one she looked up to and loved more than life, power, and the realms. She closed her eyes when she saw Seraphina had already started crying; the queen of the heavens had finally shed tears, and it was for her. "Hear what I have to say before you tell me there is another way," Aurealina said.

The gilded doors to the throne room closed then, and Aurealina knew her sister had called upon her chaos magic to silence everything in the realms so their conversation wouldn't be heard.

With a steady breath, Aurealina prepared to finally say what the fates had warned her about three hundred years ago. There would be no going back now because the one they called the deceiver would trick her into enacting the first step in his master's war.

But she was the goddess of a new dawn, and so long as there was light, hope remained, so she locked eyes with her sister. Suddenly her vision turned into a seething bright white as she looked to the side and said, "It's a lie!"

Chapter 10

Onyria

I wasn't sure what I was doing as I silently bolted out of Rhydian's chambers while he slept peacefully, but I knew I needed to escape.

Just like when it came to hunting in the enchanted forest, I used my surroundings and the cover of darkness to make my way through the castle.

I had passed a few guards with ease thanks to the all-black assemble I had stolen from Rhydian, along with a dagger, a cloak, and perfectly polished leather boots.

Please, stars above, make Rhydian understand. After that dream I had, everything snapped back into place like a horrible nightmare, and I had to get away from *him*.

Our love could never survive in this realm when it was the cause of the deaths of countless others across the universe.

I couldn't have that many deaths on my hands, especially when Seraphina had found another way after that fateful night. I spoke to her before I faced the devil of a realm that would need me more than ever when the time came.

But until then, I needed to ride to the Kingdom of Luminaria and warn the witches of the coming attack on their kingdom. I had enough provisions for three nights, but then I would need to stop by the nearest town on the other side of the mountains.

The vampires were rising, and with them, their lord and master, the one who had nearly killed me the day I spoke to Seraphina about my plans, the next time we faced, I wouldn't lose.

But until then, I needed to leave.

I smiled at myself as I shook my head. To think all it took was the compulsion to forget my old life as a guardian of the realms and the Primal Celestial of Dawn and Dreams was ludicrous, but my sister had gone so far as to give me new memories and a false life.

She had trusted Roderick with my safety, and he betrayed us. I could feel my ancient power humming to the surface, but I couldn't use it, not now and certainly not here.

I looked out from the shadows, pulling my hood over my head to obscure my face from any unwanted parties as I made my way to the stables.

It wasn't a horse I was after, but a crystal that Rhydian kept around their necks to access the portals that helped him travel.

After all these centuries apart, he hadn't changed a bit. I shook my head. Now wasn't the time to reminisce about the old days when we were happy.

When he looked entirely different.

Stars above, he was more beautiful than the day I granted him immortality so he could be with me forevermore.

To know he wanted it to end, he cleaved a hole in my chest and tore out my heart with the knowledge that he no longer wanted my gift.

But it is also understandable.

I was gone, and he was miserable. Our bond had been shattered when Seraphina took away all memories of him, of our life together, and of the one we fought to have.

But he betrayed me.

The deceiver wore a mask I hadn't seen until it was too late. Knowing that Rhydian, his father, the High King, and all vampires worked under the command of the Dark Lord was sickening.

They would dare break the balance so that they ruled over everything while the other species rotted and withered away.

Clenching my fist, dark flames swirled along the tips of my fingers, and I no longer cared that it would alert Rhydian.

He needed to know my memories were back, that I would oppose him in the war to come, and I would win.

I was fire-made flesh, the bringer of Dawn and Dreams, the mistress of prophecies and the queen of light. I would see him on his knees, burning for mercy, before I ever sat back and turned a blind eye to what his kind was doing to this realm and the others. My vision became a sea of light and darkness as the flames built around me until they rippled in dark pinks, reds, and purples, before exploding around me in waves of onyx and gold.

My auburn hair lit on fire until my flame-like hair became golden like the first rays of daylight before I took a deep breath and the flames flickered out like a dying candle. I should have known Seraphina would glamour me so that I didn't look like who I used to be, *who I am now* and who I will forever be.

It wasn't long until screams broke out as the castle crumbled around me. I strode for a horse in the courtyard when I noticed it had the crystal I'd been looking for.

It wouldn't take me to Luminaria, but it could take me close enough to get as far away from Rhydian as possible.

"So, you remember?" Rhydian's voice called from behind me.

I turned and faced him. "I do," was all I said. The gilded king stepped closer to me, and I spotted the gold and shadows swirling at his fingertips.

"You said you wouldn't leave me, and yet here you are running again," he said, and I saw the flash of his natural amethyst eyes as lighting lit the courtyard.

"Do you wish to fight me, *Nocta'felanis*?" I asked tauntingly. "You've forgotten who gave you such power over darkness and gold."

"I am not the one who has forgotten," he shot back, and with that, he raised his hands to strike, but as quick as his magic hummed to life, it was gone the next moment he took a breath.

"I am a goddess, *Rhys*, or have you forgotten how we met?" I asked curiously since he was so quick to attack his eternal bonded. He never liked the nicknames I teased him with, but I found joy in seeing him blush. It was sad to only see his cold shield and hatred pointed towards me. "I bend creatures of the night, such as you, to my will, but I don't want to fight you."

"Well, I sure do want to fight you," he seethed.

"Why?"

He glared at me then. "Because you left me."

"Only because you betrayed me for your precious master." I sighed.

The sounds of his guards screaming and the smell of burning flesh mingled in the air as I held Rhydian in place like a puppet on strings.

In truth, it was his blood I controlled, or more specifically, the mortal blood he consumed to keep himself strong, for that blood was life essence, and all Celestials could weave, bend, and destroy it.

But Rhydian's blood was even more special, thanks to our bond, my eternal gift, and his vampiric nature.

Rhydian laughed then, but it wasn't full of joy like all those other times; it was cold and sadistic, like that of a mad man. "His majesty looks forward to seeing you again, Onyria, or should I say, *Aurealina*?"

At the sound of my old name, my hold on Rhydian slipped, and it was more than enough time for him to use his magic.

A spear of pure shadow and gold shot for me as I grabbed the crystal off the horse behind me. I held my hand up to stop Rhydian's magic, but out of the corner of my eye, another spear came for me from behind, and I only had enough time to stop one. I screamed in agony as the burning sensation of being impaled scorched through my skin.

"What is this?" I asked.

Rhydian smirked. "That is centuries worth of pain that you inflicted on me in your absence, and just the beginning of what I plan to inflict on you after Cade has his way with you."

I shook my head and laughed. "You'll have to find me first," I said, crushing the crystal in my hands and watching as it transformed my body into *stardust*.

"No!" Rhydian shouted, but it was too late, and I was free of him once and for all. I had no doubt that once he got the fire under control, he would hunt me down.

But once my full power and immortality came back to me, he would be the one in fear of what was to come.

"Goodbye, *Nocta'felanis*," I said and bowed my head.

I thought I knew what death would feel like after suffering the loss of my brother Helios, but I remembered every detail of his handsome face, the golden shade of his hair and fair skin, and his bright amber eyes.

Everyone always told me I looked more like him than I did to Sera or Nyx, with my freckled face and auburn hair that always reminded Helios of fire.

In some ways, he and I were equal in power. Though he was the second-eldest Celestial and I was the youngest in our family of ancient primordial gods, it was hard to see why he favored me more than the rest.

As the first family and Celestials born from Stardust, we didn't know what a parent's love felt like, but as the youngest Celestial in my family, Sera and Helios were the closest things I had to real parents.

God, I missed my family. At least now, as I drowned in their memories, I would soon be reunited with them after my task was complete. I only wish I had the chance to tell Alistair goodbye; the mortal boy was the best part of my new life and would never be forgotten. The darkest and loneliest part of my soul wished I were granted what all the mortal girls got and dreamed of.

I wished I could fall in love and have my own happily ever after with a male that didn't seek overall dominion at the peril of others, but with my barely broken bond and the way fates worked against me, I would never be granted such love, for my soul would forever belong to the one that broke my heart in the first place. I closed my eyes and allowed the watery grave of my memories to drag me down the depths of its bottomless well.

I suddenly took in the softness of the floor I was lying on—no, not the marble floor or a courtyard. I grab something almost hair-like, but the smell of dirt infiltrates my nose.

My eyes snap open, and I find myself lying in a garden of sorts with nude statues and beautifully trimmed hedges of animals decorated with thorny vines and roses.

Is this the heaven my family and I built for immortals?

I shook my head. Of course, this was not the afterlife; my family was nowhere to be seen, and the ache and the overly loud pounding in my head suggested I was very much still alive.

I slowly rose from the ground and took in my surroundings. The sun gleamed brightly atop me, and the grass danced to the wind as it swayed back and forth with the flowers.

Upon seeing the ancient and majestic beast of my family soaring in the sky, their wings beating harsh gusts of wind against my body laid out on the ground, I knew where I was before I could speak it aloud.

As if hearing my thoughts, a voice so deep, familiar, and ethereal sounded from behind me. "Welcome back to the Court of Dreams, Aurealina."

I looked up to face the male who embodied dreams and nightmares, the one I had begged to let me go when my heart and soul belonged to another.

"Hello, Morpheus," I replied, bowing my head.

A wicked smile spread across his full lips as he said, "I have missed you, *wife*."

Epilogue

Alexei

"If we're not careful," Atreus whispered in my ear before trailing kisses down my throat, my bulging cock in one of his hands. "We'll both come tonight, little Viper."

The need to touch him, run my fingers over his muscular stomach, and taste his need for me was so potent that I reached for his waistband.

Atreus grabbed my wrists and pulled them over my head with a wicked grin on his face. "Not yet," he taunted. "You'll come only after I've fucked you."

Atreus was stroking me now. It started out slow, but the pace picked up speed as he looked into my eyes, our lips inches from each other.

Is it that obvious that I want him now?

I pouted for Atreus to let me feel him as the lighting outside illuminated my bed chamber in a dark purple hue. His touch was thrilling as he glided his free hand up the side of my leg while still holding my cock with his other, teasing what would happen if I obeyed him tonight.

"Atreus, please," I said quietly.

It doesn't take long for his lips to collide with mine and our teeth and tongues to clash for dominance. His stiff cock rubbed against me through his loosely buttoned breeches, causing me to gasp into his lips.

I was about to take full advantage of the situation when suddenly, the doors to my chambers flew open and my sister entered the room fully dressed in a gilded-plated gown. Her golden brown eyes found mine, and her thick black curls hung loose from her shoulders.

"For the love of—" she cut herself off, placing a hand over her face.

She turned to look away from us then, and both Atreus and I took that as our only chance to get our baring together.

"Why are you here, Elyssa?" I asked. "And why didn't you knock?"

Elyssa scoffed. "Are you presentable?" That was all she asked; still, her back was to us as we got dressed.

"You can look now, princess," Atreus said in that tone, which I knew meant he was nervous as he cleared his throat.

"Good, you can leave now and make sure to close the door behind you," Elyssa said, turning and facing us.

Atreus looked at me, and I nodded. "It was a pleasure, my prince," he said, giving me a wink before leaving me with my annoyingly rude sister.

We stood there in silence, waiting for the doors to close behind Atreus before either of us spoke up first. I knew my sister loved watching me squirm impatiently until someone said something, and she usually got her way, and I would break the silence first.

Today wasn't necessarily a win for her since she ruined a perfectly planned evening I was actually looking forward to all week.

"Why couldn't you have at least waited until after he made me come?" I asked.

Elyssa seemed to make a gag sound. "Don't use such words, please; it's gross."

I laughed. "You only think that because next week you will be worshipping a goddess instead of getting fucked."

Elyssa rolled her eyes, crossing her arms. "Alexei Nyxian Darkthorn, I say to the old gods and new, you will be punished for your filthy mouth one day."

Placing my hands on my hips, I laughed harder. It had been ages since I heard someone say my full name, and now seemed like an appropriate time to hear it.

"Enjoy being a virgin forever, little sister."

Elyssa's face flared, turning a bright red before she took a deep breath. "I am going to be the bigger person and ignore you," she told me.

I smiled. Elyssa hadn't been home in months. After our father passed, she devoted her life to the people of our kingdom, and now she would be a priestess for the goddess Athena.

Brushing all that aside, I focused on my sister, who now went towards the bed, and I watched as she sat down with a satisfied sigh.

"Why are you here?" I asked again.

Elyssa clasped her hands together in front of her and looked up at me. "Well, brother, to answer your question, our mother summoned me back home and said tomorrow we are to have a family meeting," she explained.

I groaned and threw my entire weight back into my enormous bed that could fit four extra bodies. I should know that since last night with Atreus and those two females was an exciting desert after such a boring and tasteless ball my cousin forced me to attend, but focusing on the task at hand, I asked, "What for?"

Elyssa was silent beside me on the bed at first and then finally replied, "Her majesty wishes for *you* to find someone."

I sighed and rubbed my temple. "Who?"

Elyssa seemed to beam with joy at my questions and said, "Her grace, the queen, Aurealina Stormblood."

The story continues in...

Hearts of Malice

About the Author

Shawn J. Romeo is a Canadian author who lives in Ontario with his mother and two sisters. He enjoys going out with friends when he's not nose-deep in a book, playing video games with his sisters, and listening to music while taking long walks.

He is writing fantasy stories set in the world he created as a child, but he is always curious about other genres like Dark Romance and Horror. Currently, his greatest aspirations are to write more stories in the world he created and buy more books until he has no space in his room.

Read more at Shawn J. Romeo's website
Follow him here:
Instagram: @therealshawnjromeo

Milton Keynes UK
Ingram Content Group UK Ltd.
UKHW030858111124
451035UK00005B/512